Man
of the
King

Man
of the
King

Janet Bennett

Author of Hidden Treasure

iUniverse LLC
Bloomington

Man of the King

iUniverse books may be ordered through booksellers or by contacting:

iUniverse LLC
1663 Liberty Drive
Bloomington, IN 47403
www.iuniverse.com
1-800-Authors (1-800-288-4677)

ISBN: 978-1-4502-9564-2 (sc)
ISBN: 978-1-4502-9562-8 (hc)
ISBN: 978-1-4502-9563-5 (ebk)

Library of Congress Control Number: 2013900530

Printed in the United States of America

iUniverse rev. date: 02/25/2013

Chapter 1

E LIZABETH HOLLINGBERRY WAS lost, but she would prefer to be where she was rather than any place in the world. Escaping mundane life within the prism of her mind, seeing colors flash through the vision in her imagination, she was reluctant to emerge even as she knew the painting was at its completion. There were no improvements she could make to this very personal gift.

Lilith Hollingberry, Elizabeth's step-mother, was her subject for the past few months to surprise her father, a splendid gift to celebrate his marriage to Lilith five years ago. To achieve secrecy they met in the small outbuilding that housed Elizabeth's passion and all its entrapments. Surrounded by Elizabeth's many canvases, painting supplies and the little cart she often used to tote her things out and about to capture her surroundings in oils or charcoal, Lilith knew that Elizabeth painted exactly what she envisioned. It didn't matter if she were standing in the middle of pigsty, she had all the confidence in Elizabeth's talents to portray her in the best way.

"This will be splendid to give to Papa," Elizabeth declared with her painting smock and dress covered in as much paint as the canvas. She beamed at her work, admiring it with more than a smidgen of pride and a sense of accomplishing something great.

Lilith was made to promise not to look at the painting until it reached completion. The suspense was positively dreadful. Now, with brazen curiosity, Lilith wasted no time making her way to the other side of the canvas.

At first Lilith could only stare. Could it possibly be? Every little nuance was captured. The sparkle in her bright blue eyes, the sheen of her blonde hair speckled with warm, natural highlights, a soft smile graced her lips and her expression was one of looking at someone she loved. Tears rolled down Lilith's cheeks unchecked. She would have forgotten to breathe if it hadn't been an involuntary function.

"This is perfection," Lilith gasped. She wanted to look back at Elizabeth as she paid her the ultimate compliment, but couldn't tear her eyes away from this masterpiece.

The background was created solely out of Elizabeth's imagination. The setting had Lilith seated in an elaborately carved, high backed chair. The magnificent details were impressive yet didn't overshadow the subject. Every shade, every color, every angle was precisely where it should be.

"Elizabeth," she breathlessly sighed, "you are an artist, for sure. I've never seen such quality."

At twenty years of age, Elizabeth reached a masterful level in her painting. Several pieces of her work could be found gracing the walls of Listhenshire Hall, as well as several other Hollingberry estates. Most of her paintings consisted of still-lifes, but now that she produced such an exquisite portrait, Lilith would have to encourage her to follow this new talent.

"Thank you," Elizabeth said confidently, "it came from years of practice." Elizabeth thoroughly cleaned her brushes and palette with care and placed them in the small cart. "I think it would be best placed above the mantel in Papa's study. He spends so much time there, it would be a waste to put it anywhere else," she said absently.

"Oh, yes. What a lovely idea, then he could both think of both of us while he gazes at it fondly. We can give it to him at the party tomorrow eve. He will be here tomorrow with Wesley if everything has gone as splendidly as Edward planned," Lilith said excitedly.

"I know this celebration we planned for Wesley's return after five years away at university will be a great success. If he wasn't your son, I'd be wondering if he wasn't the king himself for all the planning we've managed to contrive," Elizabeth said without malevolence. After all, Wesley was her only son.

Everyone was busy as squirrels gathering for the winter. The only one not put to work was Kathryn, and she was forbidden to move a muscle.

Despite social etiquette Elizabeth invited her very pregnant friend for this intimate welcoming party to help celebrate Wesley's return to the family, thinly disguised by the invitation for her husband, who knew Wesley from university, to join them.

"Is Kathryn settling in well? She did seem a little peaked when they arrived this morning," Lilith said, continuing to examine the portrait before her.

"She assured me that it was the bumpy carriage ride that was making her ill. She hasn't experienced morning sickness for some time now. As a matter of fact we are planning to have lunch in the garden this afternoon. Would you like to join us?" she asked.

"Thank you, but I must attend to some letters. I will take my meal in my room. You two always have so much to talk about that I would be in the way. You go have a good visit," Lilith said, knowing full well that she would feel like an interloper.

Placing a kiss on Lilith's cheek, Elizabeth departed toward the south side of the castle. As she ascended the hill toward her home, she began to wonder of the success she would have with Wesley. Elizabeth didn't know her step-brother very well and was quite nervous about making a good impression with him. After all, Wesley would be taking more responsibility in family affairs as was custom for sons.

She would see soon enough. Now it was time to change for luncheon. She anxiously hurried, changing out of her painting smock and dress and into finer apparel appropriate for hosting before heading to the garden to meet her friend.

Kathryn Cunninghame, the proud wife of Caleb Cunninghame of Dorset, was caught caressing her swollen belly as Elizabeth entered the gazebo.

"Oh, how jealous I am," Elizabeth crooned. Kathryn smiled and opened her arms for an embrace from her oldest, dearest friend in the entire world, excusably not rising out of her seat.

"It will be time for you some day to have a family. I can feel it," Kathryn replied.

"Not anytime soon, I'm afraid. There is a decided lack of suitable suitors in this area, especially if you ask my father," Elizabeth said with a distinct roll of her eyes.

"Take heart, Elizabeth," Kathryn consoled, "as the youngest of five girls, your father has your best interest at heart."

"Yes, I'm certain he does, but I hope he will find someone quickly, before I turn gray. I wish to enjoy being married as you and Caleb apparently are," she said yearningly.

"It is divine, Elizabeth, to marry out of love. I couldn't ask for a better man, a better life, and with the baby, I couldn't be happier," Kathryn said, knowing that her friend would share her joys.

"I'm truly happy for you, Kathryn," Elizabeth said with all the love she felt in her heart. That love crowded out any feelings of resentment and jealousy that could have moved in its place.

"Oh, look, Darwin is coming. He carries a post," Kathryn said, observing the tall, slender elderly man making slow strides demonstrating his age carrying a small silver platter decorated with a single letter.

"Two months ago I wrote one of Wesley's instructors, Professor Deventer, inquiring what would make a good gift for his homecoming. I had given up hope, thinking his reply wouldn't show until the day after Wesley's return. Maybe he finally got around to responding. After all, it is the day *before* Wesley's arrival," Elizabeth quipped.

"Have you found an alternative?" Kathryn asked.

"Yes, I settled on giving him a dagger. Every young man needs a dagger to keep at his side," Elizabeth said with conviction, "I drew a picture of what I wanted the smithy to make and he replicated it splendidly. It's a wonderful specimen if I say so myself, and the smithy earned a bonus for a job well done."

"I'm sure Wesley will have no equal to it in his lifetime." Kathryn beamed.

Darwin finally crossed the expanse of the garden in his slow, lumbering stride and presented the letter.

"It's from my sister, Taralyn. It says she, too, is with child and says she wants to visit while she can still travel," Elizabeth exclaimed excitedly.

"Oh how wonderful! I hope she has a good trip. I agree that traveling early is best. Even the short trip between our homes was enough for me, let alone all the way from Wales. Oh, don't look so downhearted, Elizabeth. Your time will come," Kathryn consoled.

"I know, Kathryn. I mustn't complain about my life, but a female can only handle so much grooming for married life, and I am well past the age of grooming. I'm practically an old biddy." The two friends laughed and carried on until the clouds interrupted their fun and they made their way inside.

Chapter 2

E DWARD WAS TO deliver Wesley soon and the house was abuzz with excitement. The entire household fed off Lilith's enthusiasm. She was absolutely bubbling with delight. She would not have to send Wesley back after holiday was over, she would not have to be separated from her son any longer. He left a boy and was coming back a man. She could hardly wait.

"They're here," Lilith urgently announced after flinging open the drawing room doors. Elizabeth and Kathryn had been patiently filling their time with some needlepoint, wisely staying out of Lilith's way. "Come! Come!" Lilith's urgency was manifest by quick gestures and a large smile. She was bordering on unladylike behavior, but Elizabeth would not fault her for the love of her son.

Lilith and Elizabeth, along with Caleb, Kathryn, and the staff were standing at the door ready to greet Edward and Wesley. Lilith waited with quiet exhilaration as Edward came out of the carriage-alone. His face was sullen and his head hung low.

"Sorry, love. He didn't want to come home," Edward's sullen words fell solid on Lilith's heart and her face fell as her heart sank to its lowest depths. Edward held a straight face as long as possible. Just as his smile broke, Wesley jumped down from the carriage and scooped his mother up into his arms.

"Wesley! That was a horrible trick to play on your mother!" Lilith scolded, then hugged him as hard as she was able. "You've grown so much since your last visit that I almost didn't recognize you. It's wonderful to have you home," Wesley put his mother on her own two feet and stared down at her.

"Yes, I believe it is," Wesley said, turning his head momentarily, caught by the vision to his immediate left. "Who is this?" he said breathlessly. Wesley put on a grand show of approaching Elizabeth, kneeling before her and kissing her hand.

"Oh, Wesley, it's just me. It has only been a year and a half since we last saw each other. I haven't changed in the least bit," Elizabeth said, rolling her eyes, pretending to be not shocked by the display of adoration Wesley was giving her. Elizabeth took note that Wesley hadn't physically changed much since his last visit, contrary to Lilith's opinion. She would have thought he would have grown a bit more in that span of time, but then he was just a boy being only eighteen years old. He could shoot up in his later years like many young males do.

"Take care, my friend. If you ignore the rest of us, you run the risk of not receiving your gifts," the note of warning deep in Caleb's voice was mocked by the smile on his face.

Wesley stood from his kneeling stance to firmly grasp the hand of Caleb Cunninghame, a man he respected. "I've not seen you at Cambridge. Have you gone on to greener pastures?"

"I've come to help my wife's family. We were told that you were released from the great minds of university and had to come celebrate your safe return," Caleb said. As he introduced Kathryn, Caleb wondered how much information reached Wesley's brain, for he was staring at Elizabeth with amazement and something else that ought not to be in his eyes. Caleb understood, for he was a young buck once, full of life and male needs. That thought diminished Caleb's smile as he recalled the days of his youth. He was sure to keep a close eye on the boy.

"Wesley, come and celebrate with us. Everyone is waiting," Lilith bubbled. After the introduction of the staff, Wesley was ushered up to his rooms to freshen while a fine meal was being laid out in his honor.

Instead of retiring into his rooms, though, Wesley walked about the house, reacquainting himself with his surroundings. He'd spent so little time at Listhenshire since his mother married Edward. This was the perfect time to familiarize himself with the lay of the house and its wares. After all, it was his home now.

The entire second floor was dedicated to living quarters. The family kept to the southeast wing. He knew from experience that the other rooms were largely unused. His rooms were at the end of the hallway. Standing outside his door, directly to his right was a staircase meant only for servant use, to his left and down about twenty paces on the opposite side of the hall where Elizabeth's rooms and the short staircase past Elizabeth's door lead up to his mother's and Edward's rooms. Striding down the hall and to his left once more he reached the main staircase leading to where all the activity lay.

His feet landed on the stones of the large dining hall where most of the commotion originated. Lilith called out directions as the servants shuffled about preparing the hall for the feast. Some were cleaning, others spreading fresh herbs on the rushes. A fire was being stoked by a small boy who no doubt brought in the pile of wood he stood beside. Edward wisely left to attend to business matters, leaving the hustle and bustle behind. Wesley wondered where Elizabeth had gone. Turning in the opposite direction of his mother, Wesley went in search for his long-lost sister.

Alas, Elizabeth was not to be found. He searched high and low, ending his hunt in the stables only to be told she hadn't been seen. Upon re-entry to the house, though, there was a long wooden table sporting a fresh bouquet of flowers just recently placed for his benefit. The flowers were of no consequence to him. His eyes espied a miniature painting.

Elizabeth.

Quick to glance about to see if he was being watched, Wesley palmed the small portrait and placed it in his pocket. Feeling as if he were ten feet tall, Wesley confidently barged onto his mother's symphony of chaos and offered his support.

At the intimate celebration dinner, Elizabeth was seated down the crowded table from Wesley. He noticed the burnt orange gown with the black velvet bodice embroidered with gold she'd changed into for his celebration dinner. He thought it accented her elegant skin perfectly. She was sitting next to her friend, and Caleb's wife, Kathryn. Wesley thought Kathryn, a pretty red-head with silken hair and creamy complexion, quite fetching despite her delicate condition, but she was no match for Elizabeth's dark beauty. Wesley was sandwiched between his stepfather and Sir Otholomew from Dunsburough, who had not been invited but was present nonetheless.

Sir Edger Otholomew was a very prominent landholder in England and known for his astuteness with money. He was also a windbag. Wesley listened for quite some time as Sir Otholomew described his involvement in all its glory. Caleb had been at court and told Wesley and some other eager listeners at university the true goings-on. It sounded intriguing to be enmeshed in the king's affairs. It reflected nothing of what Sir Otholomew was telling them. Wesley wondered if he was making it all up for his own benefit.

"Your father tells me that he wants to teach you the family business. Good thing. He's not getting any younger," Sir Otholomew said, laughing heartily.

"Why don't you impart some of your wisdom on the lad, Sir Otholomew?" Edward invited.

"Certainly, old man," Sir Otholomew said, clapping Edward on the shoulder with great friendliness neither of them felt, effectively squeezing Wesley between the two men. "My advice to you is to keep your friends close and dear to your heart-but," leaning into Wesley's ear Sir Otholomew clearly enunciated, "keep your enemies closer." Sir Otholomew chuckled at his own prowess at stating the sum of all success. "That, my boy, is the greatest advice you will ever get. Know your enemies as well as you know yourself and you will be saving yourself a hefty amount of grief. Know where they are, what they are doing, when they plan to do it and how. It will be a pain in the arse to get the information but it will pay tenfold when you can stop an attack before it starts. Cut out the bad part of the apple, so to speak."

"Very true," Edward seconded. Wesley wondered in which category his stepfather fell, friend or foe.

Sir Otholomew went on and on about his savvy business sense and ability to run his very prosperous pieces of the countryside. "Yes, I was summoned by the king himself and shall be traveling there on the morrow. He will be soliciting my advice, no doubt."

"King Henry has a myriad of advisors and counselors, Sir Otholomew. Why would he seek yours?" Wesley asked.

If it hadn't been for the boy's ignorance of the world and the pure lack of insolence in his voice, Sir Otholomew would have taken offense, but instead he answered him.

"My dear boy, when one finds himself king, one needs to have as many supporters as possible. Supporters that know about things, and about people, and about what those people are doing. Take for instance Elizabeth," the three men turned to look at Elizabeth who was engaged in a lively conversation between Lilith and Caleb, "I will report to His Majesty that she is doing quite well and growing nicely."

A flame set in Wesley that struck his eyes. "Why would the king be interested in Elizabeth?"

"King Henry likes to be appraised of all the marriageable women and any possible suitors. Does she have any?"

"No," Edward answered quickly, "no one of importance."

"Very fine, I will also inform him of Wesley's return from university and soon to find his niche in life."

"Why would he be interested in me?" Wesley placed a hand on his chest and bowed his head in mockery. "I am but a humble boy."

"King Henry likes to be abreast of the goings on from every angle," Sir Otholomew concluded.

After the meal was finished, Edward moved the gentlemen into the study for some well-deserved port, allowing Lilith and Elizabeth time to orchestrate their surprise. Taking no heed to the fact that the men would be enjoying their drink and undoubtedly talking about the coming race, the women entered the room unannounced, followed by two male servants carrying the covered painting and an easel.

"What is this?" Edward dearly loved his wife and daughter and wouldn't think of sending them away, even during this private sport of drinking. Lilith, elegant as always, drifted over to Edward for a peck on the cheek.

"We come bearing gifts. Wesley, come away from the window," Lilith said with a light, cheery delivery, "Elizabeth has a gift for both you, Edward, and for Wesley. Elizabeth, why don't you sit by Wesley?" Lilith directed the placement of the still covered painting on the gold plated easel by the fireplace.

"I wanted to welcome you with a proper gift, Wesley. I hope you like it," she said, withdrawing an elaborately carved box from her inner sleeve and presenting it to him.

"You brought me a gift?" Wesley said, staring unblinkingly, too stunned to reach for the box.

"Yes, she had it made," Lilith declared.

"Thank you," Wesley said after coming out of his momentary reverie with a lump in his throat. Taking the box from Elizabeth, Wesley placed his hands over Elizabeth's, holding them a bit too long for propriety.

Feeling quite uncomfortable, Elizabeth politely pulled her hands from his and cleared her throat without responding to his gratitude. Removing herself from her spot and seating herself on the opposite sofa beside Kathryn, Elizabeth watched on as the others gathered about Wesley's shoulders to peer into the box.

"It's magnificent," Wesley said, taking the dagger out of its case and showing all onlookers its bejeweled handle. The dagger sat heavily in Wesley's hand as he took in the ornate design. The sharpest of blades topped a roundel-inspired handle with an intricately carved vine with leaves intertwined with an inlay of jewels, all masterfully planned to match the grip of his hand. The Hollingberry family crest inlaid the butt of the handle. "I doubt I will see another of its kind, or it's equal." Wesley placed the dagger gingerly back into its case, knowing within his heart that Elizabeth boldly declared him as part of her family.

"A fine gift, let's have another," Sir Otholomew blurted before handing Wesley a smoking pipe. Caleb gave him with a pair of cufflinks made of fine gold. There was another round of drinks poured and more lively conversation before Lilith decided it was time for the big reveal. With as much flourish and dramatization as she could muster with the small crowd, Lilith presented *le piece de resistance*.

"Ladies and gentlemen, I present to you the painting artists from all around will be trying to emulate for centuries to come," Lilith said. With the flourish of a woman of the stage, she pulled the shroud off the frame to reveal its treasure.

Everyone was astounded. Edward sat back, silenced with awe as he stared into his wife's face.

"Elizabeth, is this why you and Lilith had gone into hiding?" Edward asked.

"Yes, Papa," Elizabeth admitted modestly.

"Well," he said after a moment or two more of gawking, "I'll encourage you to hide some more if you paint this well."

"Oh, Papa," Elizabeth pinked at her father's genuine praise.

Everyone took their turn admiring the painting, discussing every brush stroke. Elizabeth was used to having her work critiqued by family, but with the new elements of Sir Otholomew present, as well as Wesley and Caleb who had never seen her paintings, it made her very sensitive to any comments coming her way.

"You created a masterpiece, Elizabeth," Wesley whispered into her ear from behind. She hadn't noticed him approaching for the sake of listening to those surrounding the portrait.

"Thank you." Elizabeth said, noting Wesley's legs brushing up against her expansive skirts as he walked around to face her. He was slightly taller than she with his heeled shoes. His blonde ringlets falling over his forehead and ears reminded Elizabeth of cherubs, not quite chin length as was the style.

"You are quite the artist, Elizabeth. My mother said that you gave the smithy the design for this dagger." He said patting the dagger in its sheath already placed at his side, proudly displaying his prize. The bright colors of his sleeveless short coat and his fair complexion contrasted with the addition of the sidearm.

"It's nothing, a simple design," She said tentatively, unable to understand Wesley's attentiveness, his close proximity, and the uncertainty of his motives.

"Yes, it is simple but it only lends to its elegance. It speaks of your ample talent," Wesley's compliment was sullied by the feeling that, even though his eyes never left her face, Elizabeth was sure there was a hint of lustful thought in his comment, for his eyes spoke a different message.

Elizabeth was immensely relieved when Caleb called over to her, asking her to explain how she worked her brush to accomplish the play of light to capture Lilith's liveliness, light and drama. For the remainder of the evening Elizabeth remained startlingly attentive to the other guest's needs, allowing them to monopolize her time.

Chapter 3

"THINGS ARE HAPPENING *just as we'd planned, my love," he said with excitement.*

"Don't be too hasty to make statements of success dear. Things can change in a heartbeat. We need to act fast, though, to keep the momentum. Go on now and do what you have to do," she encouraged.

"It will be my pleasure. We may not be able to meet for a while if things go as planned, though. Are you prepared for that?" he asked, anticipating a prolonged farewell night.

"Yes, actually I am. I can't say that I like the thought, but it is a means to an end," she said in a sorrowful, sultry voice.

"Then let's make use of this last night," he suggested with a smile.

The next morning while the household slept, Lilith and Elizabeth broke their fast and discussed the previous night's happenings.

"I'm so glad Father and Wesley made the trip without event. It was a horrible trick Wesley played on you. He surely must have a wicked bone in his body, hidden away somewhere to want to give his poor mother a start like that." Elizabeth fussed as she poured more perry into Lilith's empty cup for the third time this morning. "I should insist that he come crawling to you, begging your forgiveness for such a dreadful fiasco."

"Dear Elizabeth, I can understand your feelings for me, and I appreciate your concern, but I've already forgiven him. As soon as he appeared, he was forgiven," Lilith admitted. Looking back on the occasion and imagining the look on her own face before, during and after her beloved son's antics made her chuckle. "Besides, if Wesley must fall on his sword, so must your father. He's just as guilty as Wesley for going along with the scheme."

"That is true, but we should have withheld both their gifts until next week for their devious behavior," Elizabeth scoffed.

"Are there more gifts?" Wesley said, strolling into the dining hall with a broad smile on his face. "What better gift can a man ask for than to breakfast with two of the prettiest women in all of England?" Wesley placed a kiss on his mother's cheek and bowed to Elizabeth before taking a seat beside his mother.

"We were just discussing punishment for you and Edward for that trick you subjected me to last evening," Lilith confessed.

"Yes, I must apologize. It was quite cruel of me. Will you forgive me?" Wesley asked forlornly.

Lilith glanced over at Elizabeth, intentionally prolonging his agony by suspension of her answer.

"Only if you promise never to do that again," Lilith scolded.

"Yes, Mother, I promise," Wesley agreed. Another kiss graced her cheek and a wink was sent across the table to Elizabeth. She received it with the inkling that Wesley was quite the prankster and would be causing a bit of a stir in the future.

"What are your plans for the day, Elizabeth?" Wesley asked directly. Elizabeth took a prolonged sip and pondered the wisdom of divulging her plans. Forsaking her original impression for giving him the benefit of the doubt, she decided to indulge him.

"I thought I would go for a ride. This morning is just too beautiful to ignore. I'm sure Majesty would like to stretch her legs out a bit," she said.

"Do you care if I join you, that is, if mother doesn't mind?" Wesley asked, paying no attention to Elizabeth's protest of her shaking head.

"I'm sure your mother would like to spend quality time with you, without having to share you with anyone," she objected, kicking herself for not seeing this sort of thing coming.

"No, not at all, I have some business I must attend to and you'll be back long before I'm finished. I will claim enough of his time and attention later." Lilith smiled, turning her attention to Elizabeth. "Do have fun Elizabeth. Wesley won't be at your disposal for long. Your father will be gaining the lion's share of his time soon enough."

"Good, then it's done. We'll go riding on this fine morning," Wesley said, satisfied with the direction of the morning's activities. Taking his leave before any more objections could be made, Wesley went off to change into riding gear with plans of choosing just the right horse for today's exercise.

Up in her room with Charlotte, her lady's maid, Elizabeth changed into her riding habit. Pinning her hair up under her hat, and unable to rid herself of the sinking feeling in the pit of her stomach, Elizabeth decided to engage Charlotte.

"Charlotte, what do you think of Wesley?" Elizabeth asked.

"Why, Miss Elizabeth? Is there something amiss?" the maid asked.

Charlotte had been her lady's maid for two years now. Marybeth, Charlotte's mother and Elizabeth's old nurse maid, had groomed her to be the best. Elizabeth had no doubt that she could trust Charlotte with her thoughts.

"Not so much. I just don't have that much experience with men to know how to handle them," she confessed, hoping to sound nonchalant.

"I wouldn't go as far as calling him a man," Charlotte interjected, "he's only just passed his eighteenth birthday."

"To be sure, but even so, I need to ask you to act as duenna," she said in a decisive tone.

"Duenna?" Charlotte was taken aback. "I can understand the need for a chaperon with another man, but Wesley is your brother."

"Call it woman's intuition. Something doesn't feel right when I'm around him. He's too attentive, he stands too close to me, and he acts too overly familiar with me," Elizabeth confessed, wondering if she went too far with telling the maid her fears.

"Maybe that is just his way." Charlotte said as she placed Elizabeth's cape across her shoulders. "I have a cousin like that. He says he's not even aware that he is doing it unless someone points it out to him. Maybe it's his nature to be affectionate."

"Perhaps, but I would still feel safer if you would come along." Elizabeth knew she could order Charlotte to come with her, but ordering wasn't Elizabeth's style with Charlotte.

"I must warn you that I'm not the horsewoman you are," Charlotte said, discomfited with the thought of riding with wild abandon as she'd witnessed Miss Elizabeth do so many times.

"Well noted," Elizabeth said. With that, Elizabeth waited until Charlotte changed into something more suitable than the maid's uniform for riding.

Wesley was patiently waiting in the stalls, already having chosen one of Edward's steeds for this morning's exercise when Elizabeth arrived. The combination of the compact tidiness of her habit, its color like a fresh blade of grass, along with her chestnut brown curls and fair skin made Wesley think of spring and innocents. He thought her even more beautiful now than when she first appeared at the door to greet him. His heart skipped a beat as she requested his assistance to mount while the stable boy assisted her lady's maid. Gone was the idea that she was his sister by marriage. Something possessive seized his heart.

The ride was a pleasant one. Since Suffolk was a rather flat parcel of earth, it was easy to get into a full run with her horse, Majesty, named after King Henry VIII who insisted on the title. Listhenshire Hall was known for its grand gardens and landscaped hills. They need not fear of falling into the marsh or the wetlands for which Suffolk was known for. They were to the north of Listhenshire Hall, bordering a portion of land shared by the Boulstridges. Kathryn's mother, Iris, Aunt Rose and brother, George, and his wife, Martha, still lived over the hill and by the way.

Elizabeth rode hard, making the most of the trip out of the house. She gave a cursory glance behind her to see if Wesley and Charlotte were keeping up. This was big fun. Elizabeth couldn't remember when last she had someone to race. Where the finish line was to be drawn was up to her.

An attack of guilty pleasure assuaged Elizabeth's desire to continue the game of chase. Here it was Wesley's first full day home and she had to go show off her skill as a good horsewoman, and what of Charlotte? Surely she must have a sore backside by now, for she wasn't accustomed to riding in such a manner.

Elizabeth reined in Majesty, pulling her into the shade. They both were winded yet exhilarated by the exercise. The coppice shading them was full of oak, ash, and chequer teaming with creamy white flowers. She was just about to pull a small branch from the bounty when she heard shouts.

Elizabeth urged Majesty into motion, frantic to find from whence the bellow hailed. Charlotte's voice carried urgency, repeating her cry until they were located.

"What happened?" Elizabeth cried as she viewed an unseated Wesley splayed out on the ground.

"I fell," Wesley said, stating the obvious rather bluntly. Either out of embarrassment or out of pain, Wesley didn't meet Elizabeth's eyes. Elizabeth dismounted and ran to his side.

"Where do you hurt?" she asked frantically, scanning his person for signs of injury.

"Besides my pride?" he scoffed, "the wind was knocked out of me. I'm sure if I just lay here for a moment it will return to me."

"Charlotte, go get help," Elizabeth said without compunction. Wesley would need more help than the two women could give him.

"You'll be all right," she assured him, "Lilith would flog me if she knew I was so reckless with you." Elizabeth took Wesley's hand into hers.

"It's not your fault. I must have chosen a temperamental horse. I'll know better next time," Wesley said, attempting to smile and ease Elizabeth's fears, but it didn't reach his eyes. Instead he found himself staring into her soft green eyes.

"How did it happen?" she asked, looking about for the missing stead.

"You are very beautiful," Wesley said, taking Elizabeth by surprise. She looked at him wondering if he hadn't hit his head on the way down.

"How many fingers do you see?" Elizabeth said, waving three fingers before his face and concern spread across her brow. Wesley took hold of her engaging hand, bringing her knuckles to his lips and placed his other hand to her cheek.

"I mean it. Do you know that I have a tremendous crush on you?" he asked, clearly under a lovesick spell.

Was he daft? Elizabeth was worried something must have truly injured his head for him to be talking in such a way.

"Wesley, can you tell me where you are?" she asked, growing more concerned by the minute.

"I know where I want to be. I want to be in your arms," he said. The look in his eyes was not from a man having just hit his head, but speaking clearly and concisely. Elizabeth tore herself away from Wesley, aghast from his confession. "Don't you feel the same of me?"

"No, Wesley. No." Elizabeth yelled back. She laced her arms across her middle, suddenly feeling ill, and attempted to walk off her consternation by pacing to and fro. "Wesley, this is inappropriate on many different levels."

"Love covers a multitude of sins," he said breathlessly.

"You're my brother," she fired back.

"Only by marriage," he said after propping himself up onto his elbows in attempt to test his situation. "We're not of the same blood."

"That doesn't change the fact that you are an untried youth, just out of university and two years my junior," she said, not caring if she offended him with her remark.

"You could do worse. I may be untried, but with a woman such as yourself I could be a much better man. You are twenty years old, Elizabeth, getting past the age of desirability. Soon you will have to settle for an elderly, toothless benefactor to care for you. What is your father waiting for? Perhaps he has a plan for you after all. I heard him talking with Sir Otholomew about you, saying what a shame it is that you haven't married yet. Maybe Sir Otholomew will take pity on you and offer for you while he's here," he said bitingly.

"You are horrid, Wesley. I have plenty of suitors. Papa is the one that will not agree to allow me to marry the coxcombs that have made offers as of late. He has my best interest at heart," Elizabeth said, shaking with ire.

Wesley fell back onto the ground, unable to complete the journey to a vertical stance. After a few moments of silence Elizabeth wondered if he hadn't passed out, but she wasn't going near him to find out, not after he said those vile things.

"Yes, you're right. I'm sure of it," he said, halfheartedly. "Your knight in shining armor is right around the corner awaiting his pristine child bride. Oh, wait, you are no longer a child and I doubt if you are pristine, but then no one would expect someone of your age to be untouched. I'm sure your father is keeping you innocent for a reason, for what reason I can only imagine," he said, implying a sinister scheming by Edward's hand.

"Stop it," she screamed as she covered her ears, "just stop it." Not ever will someone disparage her good name and her father's, implying such deceitful intentions toward her. She should tell her father what Wesley said, then he would receive a sound thrashing for saying such things to her.

No longer tolerating his presence, she left Wesley behind. If she would have been able to mount Majesty by herself she wouldn't have had to walk, but there were no tall rocks or tree stumps in sight. She met the party of servants sent to fetch Wesley half way back through the garden. Upon noticing Elizabeth's distress, Charlotte separated herself from the group letting the others to tend to Wesley.

Elizabeth forgot herself and spewed every horrid detail of the event to the servant, albeit she could hardly formulate the words. It wasn't difficult to understand the true happening, however.

"I wouldn't put it past him to have fallen on purpose in order to get you alone," Charlotte said, filled with righteous indignation as Elizabeth recited his words. "How dare he besmirch your good name? And to think that your father not wanting a successful marriage for you! That's preposterous! That mouth of his is going to get him killed one of these days if he doesn't learn how to control his tongue."

"Yes, I know," Elizabeth cried, feeling guilty for letting herself get emotionally overworked. "What do you think, Charlotte, am I too old?"

"Don't play into Wesley's games, Miss Elizabeth. It will only cause you heartache," Charlotte said, knowing nothing she said, positive or negative, was going to assuage Elizabeth's fears.

"How did you get to be so wise Charlotte?" Elizabeth said with a sniffle.

"From listening to my mother," she said without a second thought, "don't tell her I said that, though. She'll never let me live it down."

"I won't as long as you don't breathe a word of this to anyone. I'm so ashamed," Elizabeth confessed and began to cry.

The next day Elizabeth was able to avoid Wesley, for he was recovering in his rooms and declined joining family affairs. Elizabeth wanted to speak with Lilith about her son's behavior, but was hesitant to cause distress to her heart. She hadn't even spoken of this to her best friend of twenty years for fear of causing stress to Kathryn in her delicate condition. She would pretend as if nothing ever happened and deal with the miscreant after the Cunninghames departed for Caprington.

Chapter 4

S IR GABRIEL ATHELSTON was called to have an audience with the king. Gabriel was prepared to give him only a partial report of his investigation of the theft of a hefty sum of gold King Henry himself confiscated from the monasteries dissolved in England, but only having been on the case for a short time, the king shouldn't expect too much information as of yet.

He was ushered into the king's private chambers, left standing before the seated King Henry, who had his bad leg propped up on a stool, rubbing it as his custom. Sir Otholomew stood behind the king, saying nothing.

"Sir Athelston, you are to take your commission sooner than predicted, you'll leave as soon as you can gather your men and head out," the king said in his normally gruff tone.

"What of the present investigation?" Gabriel felt the need to remind him.

"You'll pass on any pertinent information to Thomas Cromwell. How long will it take you to be ready to leave?" the king shot back.

"With the four thousand men you gave me to command, Your Majesty, possibly two weeks." Gabriel wasn't swept with the urgency of the king's decree of early departure, but with the look on Sir Otholomew's face. His expression changed from thoughtful to a disapproving look. "If you wish, I could take a smaller band of men and head out earlier. The remainder can join us later."

"No, no. I don't think that is necessary," Henry said, almost absent-mindedly.

"I beg your pardon, Your Majesty, but may I ask what predicated the decision to move forward this soon?" Gabriel asked, watching Sir Otholomew's reaction.

"I'm sure Lord Garrott would appreciate haste, seeing that his health has declined much in the last few months. He wishes to be rid of his commission and back at his family home before winter," King Henry said as he rubbed his leg, again distracted by the pain the old jousting wound gave him. "You are unmarried, are you not?"

"Yes, Your Majesty, I'm currently unmarried," Gabriel responded after a stunned pause at the abrupt change in subject, feeling that this subject was about to cause him grief.

"Well, then, I should offer you, no I should decree you a married man as my gift to you," the king declared as Gabriel's trained expression hid his shock.

"Excuse me, sir, but I don't understand," he said, keeping careful control of his features, for marriage was the last thing Gabriel needed or wanted.

"I wish to gift you, Sir Athelston. Why is that so hard to understand? You've been in my service for ten years, with the last five guarding the throne. Now that you will be guarding my borders, I wish you to be happy doing so. Do you wish to decline?" the king asked with a raised brow and a scrutinizing glare.

"No Your Majesty," Gabriel replied calmly with a clenched jaw. With every fiber of his being screaming, he schooled himself and persevered. Declining the king could jeopardize all that he'd worked for. "Do you have someone specific in mind?"

"Yes, and I think you know her, or at least the family. Elizabeth Hollingberry is her name," the king revealed. What was more revealing was the change in Sir Otholomew. His face softened and a gentle smile came to his mouth, only to be interrupted by a slightly furrowed brow.

"Yes, I know the family. They have been my family's neighbors for many years," Gabriel said, forming his own opinion on this new subject.

"Good, great even. You will collect her as soon as you are able and take her to Piffenview. Gather your men and go fetch your wife. Have babies and guard my borders. I'm sure you will be successful at both endeavors."

With the flick of his wrist, King Henry dismissed Gabriel, sending him on his way to wonder about the security of his future.

With his world turned upside down and shaken, Gabriel kept to himself until he could bridal his emotions. His insides warred with the nagging feeling of doom as he recalled how his mother ripped their family apart. Even though he was only a small boy at the time, he vowed to himself that he would never marry, saving himself the grief of having a woman dash his hopes and dreams apart, taking with it the family fortune.

"Sir Athelston, may I have a word with you?" Sir Otholomew asked as he struggled to catch up with Gabriel. His belabored breathing was wheezy, causing him to need to rest against the wall when he finally reached Gabriel.

"Yes, Sir Otholomew, what can I do for you?" Gabriel asked the small, round man.

"I was just wondering, how long it has been since you last visited your father?" Sir Otholomew huffed between huffs of air, feeling a thin layer of perspiration collecting on his skin.

"Why do you ask?" Gabriel asked, hoping this uncomfortable discussion of his father and his condition was short and to the point.

"There have been some new developments in the area on which I would like your opinion. If we could meet, I'd love to discuss it in detail. I'm leaving for Suffolk tomorrow. I'm staying with Laurel and Hortense Beckwith, who are having a farewell party for me tonight. You are welcome to come, actually I insist. A man with one foot on the altar needs to have a little merry making," Sir Otholomew decreed with a friendly clap on Gabriel's well-muscled arm.

"Indeed," Gabriel said, feeling the pall of his mood sinking. He not only didn't feel like discussing the new acquisition of a wife, but he also didn't feel like attending any social functions either. The only aspect that piqued his interest was the news of home.

"Good, then it's settled. I'll see you tonight," he said, still huffing for his effort.

There was only one place to go to escape this madness, only one place he knew to seek consolation for his foul countenance. Gabriel strode purposefully toward The Gauntlet Tavern seeking the amber liquid it served to his heart's desire. Fortunately for him, his best friend was there to share in his misery. He pressed coin into the serving wench's palm with few words and headed toward the dark corner Bernard was known to occupy.

"What did he say?" Bernard Cabrera asked, knowing Gabriel had been summoned by the king over two hours ago. Bernard and Gabriel had arrived for service to the king within a week of each other. They became fast friends, which served them well both on and off the battlefield. They learned much about each other over the past ten years, including how to read each other's moods.

With Gabriel sitting across from him staring out into nothing, Bernard hesitated to badger his friend. This was unfamiliar territory, for Bernard had never seen him so withdrawn. Of course, there were plenty of times Gabriel had been absorbed with an investigation that it preoccupied his thoughts for a time, but this was different.

Remaining silent, displaying a vast amount of patience, Bernard nursed his pint of ale. There was no rushing the man's thoughts when he was pondering on something as weighty as his friend seemed to be.

It was well known that Gabriel was one of the king's secret weapons with his uncanny ability to ferret out and find the true intentions of people closest to the king and the throne, and as of late they have been nothing but deplorable, base intentions. Thievery, conspiracies, corruption, adultery-all of it floating between his ears and he was sick of it. Piffenview was his escape from court and he was looking forward to it. Now, though, it seemed his desire had turned on him. He was saddled with a wife, an unwanted appendage that would only diminish his joy away from court and the only life he has known for the past ten years.

"He's moved up my investiture," Gabriel finally said, solemnly.

"This isn't good news?" Bernard asked as his thick brown brows knitted together, puzzled over the lack of enthusiasm and victory over gaining the desired goal. "You've talked of nothing other than starting a new life at Piffenview for the past month. What did the king say that has changed your mind?" Bernard waited for a response, but received only a blank stare for his efforts. Bernard was flabbergasted.

In the past month, in the solitude of each other's company, Gabriel confided in Bernard regarding his hopes and dreams with the new commission of Lord of Piffenview, the border castle along the English and Scot's border. Lord Garrott, currently defending the border with only a few men, asked for reinforcements as well as a replacement. He was getting old and his health was failing. It was a perfect solution for all involved.

"I haven't changed my mind. I still want that with all my being." Gabriel said after a long, thoughtful silence. "He gave me a wife," he blurted out, unable to deliver the news any other way. Gabriel and Bernard sat silently stewing for a long while, comfortable in the silence of their own thoughts.

"Any other man would be delighted," Bernard said, knowing Gabriel's past, "but I say that you should make the best of it, or at least give it your best shot. Even if you don't come to love her, I hope you will at least like her."

"You are asking a lot, my friend. I may have to be married to her by edict from the king, but I don't have to like her," Gabriel declared obstinately.

Gabriel arrived at the Beckwith residence just after nightfall. He wanted to arrive early before the festivities gained full momentum, but he'd been detained discussing the intricacies of his investigation with Thomas Cromwell.

Ladies were finely dressed with their hair in outrageous styles while gentlemen of court followed them around hoping to gain the attention of the female of their choice even for a few moments, but no longer than a few hours.

The Beckwiths greeted Gabriel at the door, encouraging him to take his fill at the large buffet and enjoy the music, perhaps participating in dancing with one of the ladies present, but Gabriel only had one objective, to hear what Sir Otholomew had to say and leave.

"Sir Athelston, I'm so glad you could come," Sir Otholomew said, gesturing for Gabriel to sit beside him at the crowded table. A full trencher and a pint of ale were placed before him without delay.

"I didn't come for the duration of the celebration, my friend. I have many things to complete before my troupe departs. I'm sure you understand," Gabriel declined graciously and pushed the trencher away for the sake of getting down to business.

"Certainly," he replied with a fallen expression, "I pegged you from the start as someone who doesn't let his guard down very often. It seems I hit the mark. At least break bread with me. A man has to eat, doesn't he?" Sir Otholomew said as he waited until Gabriel began eating before filling his ear.

"I wanted to speak with you about some issues concerning Suffolk. It seems there have been a rash of crimes that have gone unsolved in your home town. There aren't many people in the area known for criminal activity. It is mostly country folk as you know. Gentlefolk reign."

"Yes, my father keeps me abreast of most of the goings-on in Suffolk, but he hasn't mentioned this," Gabriel said, knowing that his father only wrote of things pertinent to the estate, keeping things impersonal and distant as he always has.

"Maybe he hasn't heard of it yet, the poor man hasn't emerged from Laughtonwood for so long that I doubt he is apprised of the situation. Besides, most of the crimes are small and impersonal," Sir Otholomew said reflectively.

"What types of crimes?" Gabriel asked between bites, hoping his compliance in eating would encourage Sir Otholomew's talking, ergo shortening the time he had to suffer being here.

"I've seen destruction of personal property mostly. It seems the criminal has chosen to 'test the waters', if you will, by targeting remote areas to practice his new-found hobby. A portion of a garden was found dead overnight being scorched without fire, a forge mill was blown to bits, and a servants' housing unit was set ablaze. Every crime has escalated into a nasty trend, but no human target has been made. No one has yet deduced the culprit. We need your help to ferret out who it is before it accelerates to something much more sinister."

"I agree. Has there been loss of livestock or any wild animals found dead?" Gabriel asked, having stopped eating for the lack of appetite after contemplating the possibilities.

"Not to my knowledge, but I haven't thought to ask of wild animal remains. I'm hoping to find out who it is before it comes to that. We need someone with your expertise to find him and quick. It has gone too far as it is," Sir Otholomew said, breathing a little easier knowing that a man of his caliber was on the case. If anyone was able to crack the mystery, it will be Gabriel Athelston, the king's head investigator. He had to take pity, though, as he thought of sweet Elizabeth Hollingberry married to a man like him.

Chapter 5

E LIZABETH WASN'T ONE to sit idly by while her woes chiseled away at her. She decided to place a good distance between herself and her thoughts even if it were for a short while.

Relieved that Wesley's injuries had temporarily grounded him, Elizabeth took advantage of her brother's situation and made haste to make herself scarce. Even in his limited state, she didn't want to be caught anywhere near the repulsive brat. In fact, not even in the same household suited her fancy at this very moment.

There wasn't a moment's guesswork about where she could disappear. Mounting Majesty and riding with the speed that made her heart joyful, Elizabeth arrived at Laughtonwood in short order.

Despite his reclusiveness, Sir Athelston was quite the garden planner. His estate could rival any in beauty with its massive gardens, sculptures of the finest quality, water features that worked both to please the eye and irrigate the garden simultaneously, and most of all, the climbing vines that bloomed in almost every season covering the walls of Laughtonwood itself.

Elizabeth slowed her pace as she approached the welcoming trees that lined the entrance lane. Seemingly bowing over her in reverence and servitude, they worked to shade her from the sun and gave her free reign to quiet her distressed thoughts. It was an enchanting moment that gave her pause to breathe and reflect on her purpose in coming here in the first place.

Jumping down from her horse and straightening herself, Elizabeth imagined just what she was going to say to the poor gentleman inside. This was a delicate matter that needed finesse and diplomacy.

"Come in, my dear, it is so nice to see you on such a fine day. Did Majesty bring you swiftly?" Lincoln Athelston welcomed Elizabeth who appeared rather wind-swept.

"Yes, I'm afraid that my spirit and her legs were very unladylike this afternoon," Elizabeth said, embracing Sir Athelston and kissing his cheeks fondly. Even as the years wore on enshrouded in the depression and anxiety he kept hidden, not one wrinkle appeared on his face or grey hair on his head. His complexion seemed quite sallow, even more so as of late, but that could be explained by the hermetic lifestyle he chose, not getting out of doors into the sunlight. Still, Elizabeth felt a kindred spirit in him, some sense of connection in loss, she with the loss of her mother and Lincoln with the loss of his marriage.

"I'm sorry my dear, but I refuse to believe there is anything unladylike about you, no matter what you do. Please, sit by the fire with me. Refreshments will arrive shortly," he said, drawing her further into the room.

The two had been meeting at least once a month, more often during the warmer seasons, to talk neighborly. Lincoln, at first, thought that Elizabeth came out of pity for him and his pathetic situation, but then found that she was a delightful soul looking for kinship wherever she could. There was no prying into his personal life or inquiry that would suggest her presence had any ill motive or for any other reason than friendship. She did, though, make him feel uncomfortable when encouraging him to leave the safe haven of his home, even if for a stroll through his immaculate gardens.

"How kind of you to think of me in such a way, Sir Athelston, you would change your mind if you saw me in my painting smock and toting a cart through the marsh as I often do," she admitted with a blush.

"Yes, I certainly know that. However else would you have captured that lovely Eurasian Crane? I do say I hope my note to thank you for such a lovely gift conveyed my gratitude. I can't thank you enough for your talents in bringing to life the great out of doors to this old shut-in," Lincoln said, gathering her to sit with him by the small fire he always seemed to need as of late.

"You are very welcome. It was my pleasure. I knew that you would appreciate it more than anyone else," she said, hoping his appreciation would spring him into compliance for her next project. "Actually, that is why I came to see you today."

"Do you mean to take it back?" he asked forlornly.

"No nothing such as that. Actually, I was hoping that you would be happy with my work enough to sit for me," Elizabeth proposed, holding her breath in anticipation as he contemplated her request. "If you need confidence in my work with people, you can ask Kathryn's brother, George Boulstridge, or my step-mother Lilith. Both have sat for me with great success."

Sir Athelston was taken aback. He'd never thought that someone would take interest in him, much less want to paint his portrait after his falling out of society, but it seemed this young lady had taken keen to do just that. He had come to respect her over the past few years of their visits and didn't wish to offend her tender sensibilities with an immediate decline to her generous offer, but there was no other option in his mind.

"If you'll allow me to consider it for a time, I may be able to give you an answer, but for now let's enjoy each other's company. I hear that your step-brother has arrived home safely. How did he like your gift? It was a fine specimen if I say so myself," Lincoln said, taking note of the tension in Elizabeth's shoulders.

"He liked it well enough," she said, wanting to change topics as soon as possible. "You'll never guess who came to the party. Sir Otholomew graced us with his presence with nary an invitation."

"Ach-," Lincoln scoffed his dislike of the man, having said as much many times before, "that is so like him. He thinks he's lord of the land with the way he prances his pompous, plump behind across our fair countryside."

"Yes, but I had a chance to inquire of the unsavory happenings as of late. Even with all his investigation, he still doesn't have any idea who is doing these things or why. The crimes are as random as whom he chooses to visit them upon," Elizabeth said, just as concerned about the crimes as anyone, waiting with baited breath when her family would wake to find their property had been vandalized like their neighbors.

"Have you spoken with your father about this? What does he think?" Lincoln stood, clearly agitated with the thought of criminals running amok in his corner of the world.

"He doesn't have a clue who it might be. Lilith, on the other hand, blames it all on the Colhosters, but she blames *everything* on the Colhosters. Being half Scot automatically makes them the perpetrator in her book. I dare not tell her that they propositioned Papa to buy a portion of our land."

"Only those not in control of their finances sell property, what were they thinking?" Lincoln said without thinking of his own misfortune. Elizabeth didn't bring it to mind that they themselves purchased a track of land from him after his own debacle.

"I honestly don't know. It makes them seem presumptuous, land mongering even. It certainly doesn't seem they are acting very gentlemanly." Elizabeth adjusted her skirts, uncomfortable with the way her thoughts were headed.

"What is it, my dear? I can tell you are troubled." Lincoln regained his seat and his composure for the sake of his young friend.

"I have slanderous thoughts, Sir Athelston." She wasn't about to disparage her fellow Englishmen to just anyone. She knew that she could trust the man across from her with this, but she still didn't feel right about speaking her mind.

"Dear Elizabeth, there is a vast difference between slander and speculation. I fear that you have confused the two. Tell me what you are thinking."

"I fear that my thoughts have come to the conclusion that the Colhosters could very well be the culprits. Even though their forge mill was destroyed, it may be a ploy to draw attention away from themselves, and if that is so, who is to say that their plan is to drive others away, to encourage others to sell or abandon their property in effort to escape this criminal activity?"

"My dear, dear sweet Elizabeth, it would take much more than a few criminal acts to make people do that. Whoever is committing these crimes is after something very different." Lincoln could see the fear creep into Elizabeth's eyes and instantly regretted his statement. "They are not out to wreak havoc on the community as such, they are too inconsistent and innocuous for that. They haven't caused enough of a stir to make people want to run the other way."

"Well, it's enough of a jolt to me to want to run away." Elizabeth stood, preparing to leave being thoroughly unnerved discussing the unsettling matter of crimes within her community.

"I understand that, but I assure you that your family is safe in any instance." He wanted to assure her and settle her distressed mind. He couldn't bear the thought of something happening that would send her scattering, removing herself from him. He'd experienced that feeling before and never wanted to feel it ever again.

"I suppose you're right," she acquiesced after thinking it over, "I still don't like it. I feel very protective of my friends and family. I don't like it even if it is a perceived threat."

"I understand and respect your view. Now, why don't we have another look at that crane." Directing her away from the troubling conversation and the painful track of emotion, Lincoln lead her through the door and out toward his gallery.

Chapter 6

ELIZABETH HELD TIGHTLY to Kathryn's arm as they strolled one last time through the gardens a week after arriving. "I wish you didn't have to leave. I do so love to monopolize your time."

"As I do yours, but we must go. Aunt Rose is the only one to keep Mama company while George and Martha are away in London and I promised we would stay with her for a time." Kathryn's hand possessively caressed her swollen abdomen while she talked. "Closer to my time, if you're not otherwise indisposed, I'll call for you."

"I would be honored," Elizabeth said breathlessly, aghast with the thought of having the opportunity to help her friend usher in the next generation of Cunninghames. They embraced once more, holding tight for a little while longer, in anticipation of their loneliness apart. "I'll miss you deeply."

"Don't forget, now, that I'm just a day's walk from here or an hour at a dead run on your horse. We'll visit. Once I get set up with mother, I'll send an invitation for scones and cider." Kathryn winked, knowing Elizabeth would remember the many times an innocent invitation would turn into a week's stay. Far gone were the days of girlhood, though. They were women with families and responsibilities of their own. "Keep me abreast of all your affairs in the meantime. I expect to hear from you daily to keep me from guessing," Kathryn said affectionately.

"I will." Elizabeth released her friend to embark on her return journey to Caprington Castle.

"And remember," Caleb lovingly said, placing a friendly kiss on her forehead, "you may come visit at any time without invitation."

"I just may take you up on that in the near future." Caleb thought he heard a slight note of despair trailing behind her words.

Kathryn waved feverishly to the fading form of her friend. "Do you think she'll be all right with Wesley?" Kathryn asked, for there were no secrets between them. Even though Elizabeth hadn't confided in her out of compassion, her husband knew Kathryn would have bashed him over the head if he hadn't told her all that he knew regarding her friend.

"Yes, I think so. I had a rather productive talk with the boy before we left." Caleb recounted the scene as he examined his wife's beautiful face. Wesley was sitting at his writing desk when Caleb entered his rooms unannounced. The boy was almost insolent when it came to speaking about Elizabeth. Caleb made sure Wesley understood his boundaries when it came to his step-sister. "I don't think she'll have any further difficulties with him."

"Dare I ask what transpired between you two? That impish grin is getting me curious." Kathryn slipped off her shoes and wiggled her swollen toes. Caleb remained silent. "I suppose Elizabeth knows nothing of this conversation."

"No, I didn't grace her with that knowledge."

"I also suppose you didn't inform her parents."

"Your supposition is correct, my lady. Charlotte informed me that Elizabeth was adamant neither her father nor Lilith be told. She only confided in me because she felt someone needed to be told. The poor girl acted as though she was committing high treason coming to me."

"It is a sign of good loyalty, my love. Did you make sure others knew?" Kathryn never doubted her husband's sense of honor. He would never knowingly allow harm to befall her friend.

"A select few male servants were informed of the situation. They'll work quite nicely," he reassured her, "if anything comes about, they know what to do."

"Well then, we'll just have to see what kind of man Wesley turns out to be." Kathryn settled back into the cushion, placing a hand at the height of her abdomen feeling rather queasy. "At least she doesn't have far to go if she needs sanctuary."

Later that day, Elizabeth occupied herself with some needlepoint as Lilith read Geoffrey Chaucer's 'The Canterbury Tales' aloud. Lilith loved to read, and Elizabeth loved to listen to her well-educated tongue. It was rare to find such educated women, but Edward insisted she learn to read when he married her. It was a daunting task, but with the tutors and Elizabeth's assistance, she finally achieved high marks in the written word.

Elizabeth was lost in 'The Squire's Tale' when Wesley entered the room. How apt, she thought to herself. Chaucer wrote of a man bearing gifts, one of which was a mirror which allowed one to know the minds of friends and enemies alike. Elizabeth wished such a mirror existed to spare her this misery of not knowing the true intent of her stepbrother.

"Welcome, Wesley, I was wondering when you would rejoin the family. How are you feeling?" Lilith asked.

"Better. I'm still a little stiff, but that will disappear in time, I suppose." Wesley walked as if he were an old man still, holding himself gingerly and lowering himself into the chair opposite Elizabeth with care.

When Lilith resumed her reading, Elizabeth found it difficult to maintain concentration on the reading and her needlepoint. She stuck herself twice but refused to set it aside for fear of not having a buffer for her eyes, for she knew if her eyes hadn't been trained on her board she would have no recourse but to make eye contact with Wesley. She still felt the sting of his words and was unwilling to show him how much he unraveled her.

Unfortunately, a tray of refreshments was delivered, interrupting Lilith's reading. It was difficult not to betray her feelings. Unused to veiling her emotions, Elizabeth found it exhausting to do so now. Lilith provided the idle chitchat throughout the mid-day respite, but ended up throwing Elizabeth on end when her conversation landed directly in her and Wesley's laps.

"Elizabeth, I just realized that you and Wesley would make a good looking couple."

Elizabeth choked on her wine. Wesley, who was two years her junior and a penniless boy who just stepped out of the classroom, hadn't yet proved his worth or made a name for himself. He lacked all the necessary qualities a woman was looking for in a mate. She involuntarily looked straight at Wesley, who seemed just as stunned as she to hear those words spouting out of his mother's mouth.

"Really," Lilith added, "it isn't completely unheard of to marry someone close in age. You're both attractive individuals and you seem to get along," Lilith continued through Elizabeth's coughing, "Elizabeth, are you all right?"

"Yes, I'm fine. The wine went down the wrong way." Conversation ceased to exist after that. No one knew how to recover from such a statement. Finally, Lilith excused herself leaving Elizabeth alone with Wesley.

A long, awkward silence ensued.

"I want to apologize," Wesley began tentatively, leaning forward and resting his elbows on his knees, "I acted atrociously. I understand your contempt of me." Elizabeth listened as Wesley attempted to repair their wounded relationship. "I should have never said those despicable things to you."

The only weapon she felt she could employ was silence. She listened intently as Wesley began rattling on, justifying the reasons for his actions.

"Please forgive me, Elizabeth. The thing is, if I'm allowed to speak frankly, I feel a fondness for you that I have felt for no other. I've felt this way for a long time, several years in fact. You've always treated me with such warm-heartedness that I thought you felt the same for me."

Elizabeth thought hard on the matter, weighing her words with utmost care, for she didn't want to lead the boy astray. "I'm sorry that you thought I carried romantic inclinations toward you, Wesley. I thought I was treating you how a sister treats a brother. Honestly, Wesley, there was no intent to mislead you." Wesley knew she felt she spoke the truth for he heard it in her voice. Feeling restless, he abandoned his seat and crossed the room to stare blankly out of the window. "I accept your apology," she finally stated, knowing he needed the release "but I must warn you that no other such instances must occur."

Wesley didn't respond. She didn't press him for acquiescence just yet. Elizabeth was half way through her second glass of wine before he returned to his seat, addressing her limitations. "I promise not to speak of this again." His assent seemed a bit too bright for the occasion, but Elizabeth accepted the assurance. "Now, let us be rid of this depressing talk. I've been told that the Lowsleys are holding their annual country gala next week. Are you planning on attending?"

"Yes, I am." Elizabeth felt a little off kilter with the change of subject.

"Then you will have to save me a dance. I'm asking as a brother, I assure you." Wesley's smile and jubilant behavior was quite a change, auspiciously so. Maybe this was a precursor to an improved Wesley.

"I shall. Only one, though," she said with some reservation.

"I look forward to that one dance." Wesley made an excellent bow and excused himself, leaving Elizabeth to analyze the past half hour in solace. She wondered if the Lowsleys would fall out of form and have dancing at their party rather than their usual entertainment, which was in the form of plays. The Lowsley's daughter, Corrine, was of the theatrical nature but forbidden to join an acting company at the behest of her father. So, she worked on mastering her talent before gentlefolk of the country.

Elizabeth wondered if she would have any more altercations with Wesley. He seemed to have taken her expectations seriously.

Chapter 7

"*H*ave you heard *anything yet?" she asked, hoping to have any sign of their progress.*

"No," he replied without holding back his disappointment.

"What is the next move then?" She wasn't one for delayed gratification.

"Don't worry, we have time. Have you been doing your part?"

"Yes, I've done my part," she said acerbically. "I'll keep working on him. Until then, we have to have a backup plan just in case he doesn't do what I ask."

"I'm working on it. Believe me I have a fool proof plan."

"You look splendid, my lady," Charlotte said with utmost certainty, proud of the creation sitting atop of Elizabeth's head. Each curl was elegantly designed, draping across her shoulders, not a single strand out of place. Charlotte applied the perfect amount of rouge cosmetic to Elizabeth's becoming complexion.

"Thank you, Charlotte. Didn't this dress turn out perfect? The seaming and color was an excellent choice."

"Yes, I do agree. Mrs. Evans has a talent with the needle." Charlotte stood back as Elizabeth fancied herself in the full-length mirror. "This fabric, too, was a fine choice if I say so myself. It would have been a disaster to put you in anything but bold, rich colors."

"Yes, I guess that is the joy of having older sisters who insisted on the height of fashion. I forgot how hideous I looked in muted colors."

"Miss Elizabeth, you could never look hideous in anything!"

A knock at the door interrupted them. The carriage had arrived and everyone was ready to leave. Elizabeth made haste to join her family at the front door. She was the last to climb into the carriage and found herself seated beside Wesley, which was no surprise. What had been a surprise, though, was how immaculate his behavior had been in the past week. He had acted cordially toward her with no inappropriate conduct. He kept his distance and there were no further declarations of love. Elizabeth wondered if he had come to terms with the situation. She sincerely hoped he had. Maybe he will find a girl of interest at the Lowsley's party tonight, she thought. She would have to offer her support to him if he were to find a good prospective wife. It would take time before he would be ready to marry, though.

"Wesley tells me you saved a dance for him," Lilith broke the silence, obviously trying to start conversation in order to endure the two-hour journey.

"Yes, that is true. I've promised him one dance. What of you two? I haven't seen the two of you dance in some time."

"We are up in years and not quite as nimble as the likes of you, Elizabeth." Edward chimed, feeling every bit of sixty years old.

"I don't plan on dancing the night away. My energies will be focused otherwise. I hope to introduce Wesley to quite a few people and he will have a good base of acquaintances after we've made the rounds." Elizabeth had every intention of steering him into the arms of any other female besides herself. She felt obliged to introduce him to eligible girls that may, in time, need to achieve the goal of a profitable marriage. To be forewarned is to be forearmed, as they say, and Wesley would need an insider's view on the matter.

"You would do that for me?" Wesley inquired, impressed at her unsolicited offer to go to such lengths as to give up her night of pleasurable fun to spend time introducing him to the country folk, her personal friends.

"Yes. Why not? You *are* family and you can't very well go around introducing yourself to everyone you meet, especially females, without someone knowing a bit about each one, now can you?"

"Not likely. They did teach us etiquette at Cambridge," he said, "thank you. I'll pay you back in kind someday."

"I'm not doing it for selfish gain, Wesley. I simply wish to do my part to help ease your assimilation into society. Now that father has taken you under his wing, teaching you how to master running the estate, it will serve you well to have resources within the community in which to conduct business."

"How did you get to know all this?"

"What, you think all I've been doing whilst you were off at university, skipping about and drinking milk? I'm not a child, Wesley. I've been able to run the household for some time now. It was part of my training as well. I will have my own household to run, in due time, and father and Lilith trained me just as you will be trained."

"Well, one thing is for certain. My wife will have no need to lift a finger when I get married." There were chuckles all around.

"Dear boy," Edward chimed, "it has nothing to do with polishing silver or scrubbing floors. A woman can command a house very efficiently without having to lift a finger. Actually, the servants are glad of it. If the mistress of the house is a good governess over her household, the servants will look to her for direction and not flail around with indecision."

"You want a woman at your side that can make decisions without asking you every time something comes up. That will leave you free to concentrate on making a success of the properties, someone like Elizabeth, or I should say someone with Elizabeth's talents, would be able to run the household without a second thought," Lilith added, "Edward, why don't you allow Wesley some time out of your day to spend with Elizabeth and learn how a proper house is run?"

"No, that is not my intent just yet. I want him to concentrate on business for the time being. Besides, he will only have to learn it if he doesn't find a suitable wife *and* doesn't have a good steward at his disposal *at the same time*." It was true that running a household fell to the duty of the woman of the house. Men rarely did such things as choose weekly meals, plan galas, settle disputes between the staff as well as see to their health if need be. It was possible that Wesley would only incidentally learn of these things by being observant and by exposure to such mundane tasks. It was beyond mundane, to Edward's estimation, to give even a smidgeon of the boy's devoted time to such matters. Yes, pure poppycock, he thought.

"I wouldn't mind learning those things, at Elizabeth's side, of course," Wesley said shyly.

Elizabeth couldn't help but wonder if Lilith wasn't still trying to pair her and Wesley together, finding ways for them to spend time together in innocuous settings so as not to raise alarm. Quite possibly, though, she was making more out of this than need be. Lilith was just a mother looking out for the best interest of her son. She would give Wesley the benefit of the doubt and give him a second chance. After all, he had been behaving himself.

Chapter 8

W HEN THEY ARRIVED at the Lowsley's home, Lilith was found fussing over Wesley, giving him last-minute instruction and inspecting his attire like a child. Edward defended Wesley, feeling embarrassment for him. "Lilith, he's eighteen years old. He'll be fine." Edward physically turned Lilith around to redirect her attention. After placing her hand at his arm, they began heading toward the front door.

"Have you ever escorted a lady to a ball?" Elizabeth inquired. Wesley slightly shook his head, embarrassed again by his inexperience. "Don't worry. Take my lead and you'll be fine."

Elizabeth and Wesley walked up the stairs and waited to be announced. "Now, when we are announced, we wait at the top at the steps until both our names have been stated." They moved up in the line as people were introduced and allowed into the crowd.

Just before stepping into the foyer to be introduced, Elizabeth prepared to take hold of Wesley's arm, but found her hand being clutched instead. This was not permissible. Even married and engaged people didn't hold hands in public. It just wasn't done. Elizabeth found herself panicking.

"Wesley, let go of my hand." The response she received from her plea and tugging of her hand was a tighter grip. She looked at him, wondering what was going through his mind, only to find him staring out over the crowd. Could he be so fearful that he was unaware of his actions?

Despite the warning Elizabeth stated about the crowd, Wesley seemed to be unprepared for the amount of people. There were several hundred present. He stood as regal as possible, holding his shoulders straight, and tried to act unaffected. Elizabeth's only clue that he had fears was the uncomfortable grip surrounding her hand. Even with her glove on, she couldn't wiggle free. Elizabeth feared what he would do in the next few minutes, being surprised once again.

After both their names were called, a large banner was raised and confetti went flying from every possible direction. The crowd shouted, "Welcome home, Wesley!"

"It's a party for me? I would have never expected this," he said to Elizabeth, smiling from ear to ear, not releasing his grip one iota.

"You didn't think we were going to just have a few sparse friends over to celebrate your homecoming, did you?" Lilith came over to hug her bewildered son, allowing Elizabeth to finally escape Wesley's clutches. "I confess to being selfish. I didn't want to share you with the entire town at first, so we planned this party for two weeks after your arrival so you wouldn't become suspicious."

"This is Mr. and Mrs. Lowsley, our hosts tonight, and their daughter, Corrine," Elizabeth introduced them, placing herself behind Wesley so he could stand beside the lovely young lady.

"Thank you for making me feel so welcome," he said, gratefully shaking Mr. Lowsley's hand.

"It is the least we can do. Lilith and Edward are dear friends of ours, so when they asked if we would help throw this surprise party, we couldn't say no. It sounded like too much fun to pass up." Eleanor Lowsley was as gracious as she was beautiful. "I hope you enjoy yourself tonight."

People from the crowd were approaching Wesley for introductions. Elizabeth was tested to the limits in her powers of recall with some of them, but maintained her ability to stay level headed with the amount of people present. At least Wesley hadn't attempted to hold her hand in public again. Anger lingered at his crassness, dampening her mood.

It was several hours before the introductions ceased and dinner was to be served. From the corner of her eye, Elizabeth noticed one of the younger girls staring over at Wesley, whispering something to her friend of the same age. Elizabeth leaned into Wesley just enough to let him know what was going on.

"Keep those girls in mind. Even though they are only fifteen and sixteen years old, they come from good families."

"I'm not interested at the moment," he said, barely affording them a glance.

"I suppose it's just as well. You'll have plenty of time to choose a wife after you get yourself established and experience life outside of the university," she said keeping her voice low.

"That wasn't what I meant," he whispered back. Elizabeth looked over at him and felt his hand near hers. In an effort to dissuade his next unapproved action at the dining table, Elizabeth placed her hand on his forearm and allowed him to direct her to her seat.

Had she been wrong in gauging his reform? Had his motives for being improper by holding her hand in front of the crowd been intentional? Thoughts swam round her head as she took her seat. She felt flushed with anger and embarrassment.

Wesley was seated between Corrine and Elizabeth and across from Edward, Lilith, and a man named Christian Dissanayake whose wife, Bethany, sat next to Elizabeth who knew them well and had hoped to use the couple to effectively ignore Wesley's attention. The task was not an easy one.

During dinner, Wesley gently caressed the inside of her arm to gain her attention. It was a thoroughly sensual act meant to send a certain message. She instantly pulled her arm away, sending her own message. After dinner, wine and deserts were served. Her choice was the chocolate cake.

"Oh, how I adore chocolate," she said to Bethany, "I could eat it for every meal." She relished every bite. When she was finished, though, she found it almost made its way back out of her stomach when she felt Wesley's hand on her thigh.

"I also chose the chocolate cake, but am unable to finish it. Would you care to have the rest?" His hand lingered there while he posed his question.

"No, I wouldn't. Please remove your hand before I place my fork through it," she managed to say through clenched teeth. Wesley conceded, albeit languidly, with no sign of trepidation in his eyes.

If that episode weren't trying enough, contrary to past times, the Lowsleys offered dancing for entertainment. Elizabeth refused to dance, putting Wesley off with complaints of feeling sluggish after eating so much. Another hour went by and Wesley approached her again.

"You've had plenty of time, Elizabeth."

"Yes, I have, thank you." She remained seated.

"Will you dance with me, Elizabeth?" he asked, holding out his hand.

"Why should I?" she wanted to push him away.

"You wouldn't go back on your word, would you?"

"My word? What about yours? There were supposed to be no more instances like before," she shot back, acutely aware of those around her.

"All I promised was that I wouldn't speak of my love for you, to profess my feelings for you. You, on the other hand, promised me a dance. I've held up my end of the bargain, will you?" His hand remained before her as she contemplated her options. She rationalized that was going to be out on the dance floor with at least fifty other couples. She would be safe.

"All right, but there better not be any improper behavior from you," she said, comforted by the fact that the dance was the Estampie, which was one that required no touching in the least. They would be hopping about, stomping their feet, not coming into close physical contact.

"Oh, look. Elizabeth is dancing with Wesley." Lilith pointed out to Edward. "Why don't we join them?"

"Maybe in something less vigorous, my love." Kissing her hand and leading her to the punch table to bide him some time away from the dance floor. He wasn't as young as he used to be. A dance like the Estampie could hurt a man of his age.

"Don't they look cute together, Edward, our children dancing and having fun?" Lilith asked. Edward looked over at Elizabeth's smiling face, hopping about with more energy than he could ever remember having.

"Yes, dear, they are having a good time. Your goal has been achieved." He handed Lilith a cup of punch and waited until the next, much slower dance became evident.

Elizabeth was able to relax on the dance floor. She was having fun as she performed the necessary steps to complete the simple dance. She felt as if she could do this all night. Before she knew it she was laughing aloud, letting herself be free of any stress or entanglement.

Wesley was acutely aware of every move Elizabeth made. He was entranced by her. Watching her enjoy herself, dancing with delight, laughing merrily nearly caused him to break conformity and pick her up, carry her out of the hall, and take her home where he could have her to himself. He was sure she felt it, too, although she showed signs of fighting it, possibly because she was bred for propriety. She took him under her wing, she held his hand before all those people, and she leaned into him when she spoke with him. Now she was dancing with him, sharing her joy with him. It was quite possibly the best homecoming gift he could have ever received. It was more than he could have ever hoped.

It was disappointing when the music ended. He was having such a good time dancing with Elizabeth. She placed her hand on his forearm to be escorted off the floor, but he didn't want it to end. He intentionally tarried, making their exit off the floor uncomfortably slow in effort to suspend the inevitable.

"Wesley, Elizabeth," Lilith said waving at them across the room with Edward in tow, heading toward the dance floor. "Come dance with us," she pleaded as she moved closer, "it's the Ductia."

"I don't know how to dance the Ductia," Wesley stated unabashedly.

"That isn't a problem. Elizabeth will teach you, won't you Elizabeth?" Lilith beamed with a hopeful smile, pulling a reluctant Edward to the floor.

So much for avoiding close contact with Wesley tonight, she thought. Elizabeth tried her hardest to concentrate on teaching the steps to the simple dance rather than the way Wesley was touching her. She wanted to pull away. He was beginning to make her skin crawl with the looks he was casting her way.

"Now place the outside of your right foot to the-" she began only to be rudely interrupted.

"You dance extremely well, Elizabeth," Wesley said, interrupting her instruction.

"You would too if you just listen and follow instruction." Elizabeth's head began to hurt. "Now place your foot as I am." She was looking down, intentionally avoiding eye contact and prohibiting any chance of personal conversation.

"Would you like to go onto the terrace where there aren't so many people to watch my clumsiness?"

"No," she said sternly. She wouldn't have a chance against him if she were to place herself in such danger. She couldn't even stand the thought of being alone with him, even with a crowd of people surrounding them as they were now.

"Please?" he asked, punctuating his desire to be with her somewhere other than on the dance floor in that moment in time by pulling her body closer to his.

Elizabeth had enough. There was an extent to how much she could take and she had reached it. Elizabeth stepped back from Wesley, dropped her arms and gave him a glare that told him exactly what she thought of him, and promptly turned on her heel and left the dance floor. She wasn't going to be subjected to such abuse. Not from her stepbrother, nor from anyone else.

"What was that all about?" Lilith found Elizabeth in the baily some minutes later. Elizabeth was still seething, but she didn't want to air family misgivings in public.

"Nothing, I've a headache that is threatening to flatten me."

"Oh, dear, maybe you should take the carriage home and take one of Marybeth's tonics and lay down." Lilith placed a reassuring arm about Elizabeth's shoulders. "Perhaps all this excitement and activity was too much."

"Perhaps," Elizabeth conceded out of convenience. Selfishness propelled her into taking the proffered carriage, of course, at the insistence of Lilith and her father, assuring her that they would find their way home.

Just as the door of the carriage was being closed, Lilith called out and the door swung open. "I think it is best you don't ride alone. Wesley will go with you."

Elizabeth wanted to cry.

"But he's the guest of honor. He can't leave so early," she argued.

"We'll explain. Don't worry, Elizabeth, everything will work out just fine. You just lay down and you'll be home before you know it." Lilith signaled to the footman to close the door. The jerk of the horses setting the carriage in motion was enough of a jolt to bring her eyes around to Wesley.

"Why did you do that?" she asked accusingly.

"Mother didn't want you traveling home alone."

"You know what I mean, on the dance floor, at the table, or holding my hand when we arrived. Are you trying to tarnish my reputation, Wesley?"

"No," he said softly, trying to sound innocent, "that was not my intention."

"What was your intention?" Elizabeth began to feel the pressure build up behind her eyes and radiate to the back of her head. Her hands instinctively cradled her head. A tear slid down her cheek.

"Lay down, Elizabeth. We can talk about this later." Elizabeth didn't argue. She had never had such a pain in her entire life. The stress of Wesley's presence was too much. She needed to be rid of him.

Darwin was still awake and about when they arrived home. Noting Elizabeth's distress, he called for Charlotte and her mother, Marybeth. The women put her to bed and gave her a tonic. Charlotte stayed with her through the night.

To Wesley's chagrin, Charlotte stayed by her side from that moment onward. Elizabeth took the whole next day to recover, confining herself to her rooms, only allowing her maid admittance. He wasn't sure if Elizabeth told her what had transpired the previous night, but it was evident from the day he'd declared his love to her that she wanted to never be caught alone with him. He watched from the doorway of the receiving room as Charlotte stayed close by even when friends came calling. It would not do to have Charlotte around in order for his plan to work. No, it certainly had no allowances for maids.

Chapter 9

"A POST SIR Hollingberry." Darwin handed the missive to his master and quickly departed after the customary dismissal of a grunt was issued.

Edward was taken aback at the sight of the royal seal plainly set in purple wax. Perplexed at the reason the secretary of the king would be writing him, he stared the post confounded before presence of mind took hold. He read the missive and felt his lifeblood leave him.

Landing in his seat with a plop, Edward sat speechless for a long time. How could King Henry do this to him? Elizabeth was the last of his five children, and by happenstance was a carbon copy of her mother. There was no hiding his affinity for Elizabeth and the reason why. His knee-jerk reaction was to decline the king's request, but knew that this was no request. How could he lose the only connection he had left with his sweet departed wife without refusing the king?

"Hello, dear, I've been looking for you. Have you looked over my plans to renovate Hasting Hills?" Lilith asked as she sauntered over to Edward, becoming concerned as she noted his pallor had grown sallow.

"In Chlemsford?" he asked, dazed and flustered in his own misfortune.

"Yes, dear, Hasting Hills in Chlemsford. Are you feeling well? Do I need to call Marybeth to see after you?"

"Yes, yes, I'm fine. I just need a moment." Edward slipped the letter in his pocket. He didn't want to share this unfortunate news with anyone just yet. He needed to be alone with his misery until he felt strong enough to share it, and his daughter, with the world.

Dinner was quiet that evening. Tension and disquiet ran rampant through the air. Each moment of silence ground itself deeper onto Edward's nerves.

"Elizabeth, I've notice you haven't visited your painting barn lately." Edward began, making her jump at the mention of her name, "are you having a hard time deciding on your next object to paint?"

"No," the simple, quiet reply bothered Edward.

"I remember when you painted every single day." He studied her as she pushed her food about the plate with her fork. "Have you painted since finishing Lilith's portrait?"

"No sir. I haven't found the inspiration." Elizabeth put a piece of goose in her mouth to dissuade her father from asking any more questions.

"I would love to have a recent picture of Wesley, my dear," Lilith suggested, "the last one was right before your father and I married. Maybe you can paint his portrait while you find your next inspiration. You did such splendid work on mine, I'm sure you will be able to capture Wesley in his true colors."

Elizabeth refused to look at Wesley for fear of blurting out her antipathy toward him. She smiled at Lilith as she chewed the food that suddenly became distasteful. It took mammoth-sized will power to swallow it.

"I plan on traveling to Caprington soon. Kathryn has invited me to attend her and I wish to be there for the birth of her child. I doubt if I'll be able to devote any time to that task before then."

"Yes, I recall how long it took you to complete mine. At least you two won't have to hide yourselves away in secrecy." Lilith gave Edward a wink, reminding him of the pains they endured to give him the perfect gift, but there was no response from her husband. "Edward, are you sure you feel well? You look nearly ashen."

Edward's meal sat heavy in his stomach, not allowing him to enjoy any fare placed before him. Even his wine tasted sour. He realized that he had limited time to address the issue of Elizabeth's marriage to Lord Athelston. The newly titled man was coming for her with plans to take her away to a faraway place. He could barely stand it. There were no words he could form to tell her, no amount of explanation to cover his heartache. He gazed at his lovely daughter and took his own advice to remain silent until he had no other recourse.

"Elizabeth, would you care to join me for a stroll after dinner?" Edward asked.

"Yes, Papa, that would be nice. A bit of fresh air would benefit us both." Elizabeth, also noting the change in her father, became quite concerned.

They met in the gazebo overlooking the pond. The moon was full and bathing everything in its crisp beams. They stood in comfortable silence as they looked over the gardens, admiring the contrast of the night's darkness and the moonlight that created an alternate view of the botanical beauty.

"I still remember how painstakingly your mother worked at planning and implementing this garden. She was a stickler for detail. I guess that is where you get it from. You were both artists, she with her gardens and you with your paints," Edward said.

"Yes, she was. I remember when she was teaching me how to needlepoint. I ripped out more stiches than I placed because she knew they wouldn't fall right and make the sample look dreadful in the end."

"Yes, she was always far sighted in that respect." He swallowed and tried to make himself say it, to tell her she was going to be ripped out of his life just like her mother.

"I tried to paint her a couple of times," she said, trying to keep the longing out of her voice, "but after a while I forgot the details."

"My dear, there is no remembering about it. All you have to do is look in the mirror. There are many times when I catch myself looking at you, still sick over losing her." Edward had to compose himself before blubbering like a baby in front of his daughter. There was no having her see him lose his composure.

Elizabeth remained silent, knowing that what her father was confessing had been the backbone of why so many suitors had been turned away. There wasn't anyone good enough for his little look-a-like, no one suitable to remove the last vestige of his by-gone marriage. Their vows may have said "'til death do we part", but his heart will forever remain with his first love. It was heart-warming to know that such love existed between two people, right out of the story books.

"I'd like to see those portraits sometime," he said, not knowing what else to say in his torment.

"I'd like that. I'd have to look for them. I'm sure I packed them away in the west wing somewhere."

"It's a pity I never made room for your passion. I should have made a studio for you in the main house," he said, thoughtfully. "I could have built you a suitable cottage that brought you the best light."

"Yes, I'm sure you would have, but most of my paintings are out of doors."

"But it would be beneficial to you if you began painting portraits, is that not so?"

"Yes, but I hadn't planned-."

"Then it's done. My next project will be to build you a studio, a studio where people will come from all around and seek your talents. You will be sought after by everyone around. You'll have everything you need." Edward went on and on until he had Elizabeth laughing at the decadence he promised, reaching into the impractical and ridiculous.

"Why would you ever do such a thing?" she asked, never having seen him in such a mood before.

"Do I need a reason? Well, then, the reason is because I love you and I never want you to leave me." Edward misspoke and wished to withdraw his words as soon as they escaped.

"Oh, Papa, I'll never leave you. I'll always be there for you when you need me," she said, not realizing his meaning.

"Really, do you mean that?" he asked, knowing she was a woman of her word.

"Yes, of course I do. Whenever you need me, I promise to be here for you." She didn't quite understand her father's reasoning and wondered if he'd succumbed to feeling older or not feeling well and became concerned. "Why don't you allow me to walk you back into the house where you can rest? Are you sure you are feeling well?"

"No, I guess I'm not quite myself as of late. Perhaps you are right, I just need some rest." He lingered about, delaying entrance back into the house, still not ready to let her go. It warred within him fiercely. He couldn't have been any more taxed if he'd been engaged in hand-to-hand combat. He would fight to the finish, even if it were the death of him.

Chapter 10

"I COULDN'T HELP but overhear your father talking with you about his plans," Wesley stated from his doorway just as Elizabeth was reached her rooms. She let out a sigh as she looked over at him, not concealing her ire over his behavior.

"I'm sure. Good night, Wesley." She dismissed him, turning her back to him and heading into her rooms. She hadn't noticed him scurry over to her door and enter behind her.

"I do say, it is a good night. Why don't we take a stroll of our own?" Wesley was nonplussed by Elizabeth's startled reaction.

"Get out of here, Wesley. You are not welcome in my private quarters." She pushed at him to leave, gaining ground toward the door.

"All I want is a little time to get to know you," he said.

"You are well out of line coming in here, Wesley." She was agitated more than she'd ever been with anyone in her life. This was not a good start to a familial relationship, having a pest for a step-brother.

"Alright, alright I'll leave," he said, straightening himself, then turning to Elizabeth, he brought his hand to her face for a gentle stroke only to have it slapped away. Anger gripped him at the effrontery. Gripping the back of her neck, he tried to kiss her, only to get her cheek. She fought him, pushed at him, but he was stronger and it fueled his desire for her.

He hadn't planned on going this far with her, but he was caught up in the need for her, caught up in the need to carry out his desire for her. She struggled with him, but didn't call out for help, allowing him to conclude that she really wanted his attention but unable to voice her baser desires. Driven by his needs, he began pulling her away from the door and further into her private chamber when he was stopped cold.

Wesley was sopping wet from the waist down with one of Elizabeth's maids standing behind him apologizing profusely for the mishap. She was spouting something about not seeing him around the corner and she was ripe for punishment, pleading for mercy.

With his plans thwarted, Wesley returned to his rooms steaming in his own humiliation. He made his way to the wardrobe and opened it. Standing before her image, Wesley lit the two candles flanking either side. A single red rose from the garden below her window lay perfectly at the foot of the frame. It took him a few moments to calm his anger. Closing his eyes, he took in several deep breaths, blowing them out slowly through pursed lips.

Calm now, he stared at her picture. It was a recent picture, a miniature. She painted it herself, or so he was told by his mother. She was an apt artist. She painted herself with a muse-like smile and a beguiling look. She was looking directly at him with those eyes of green. He slowly peeled off the wet clothing, imagining the day when she would be his.

The maid would have to pay. Nothing would stand in the way of him gaining the object of his desire.

Nothing.

Elizabeth was fed up with Wesley, weary of his constant attention to her every move and especially the physical attention he was attempting to pay her last night. She would have to approach Lilith and inform her of the activity of her son. That was not an easy or pleasant task even to think upon, but it had to be done. She had to steel her reserve even as she sent for Lilith to come to her rooms.

"Good evening, dear, it is nice to have a quiet respite in your rooms for a change. We should do this more often," she said as she settled in the seat opposite of Elizabeth,

"I wanted to speak with you about something, Lilith. It's something that needs to be said. It's about Wesley," she said.

"What about him?"

Elizabeth told her about what happened while they went riding, explained to her what happened at Wesley's surprise party as well as the conversation at the Lowsley's. She concluded with the escapade the night before.

"I can't help but feel that things are getting out of hand," Elizabeth confessed. Lilith gently replaced her goblet of wine after contemplating everything Elizabeth said.

"I see," Lilith replied, pursing her lips, "I think I know what the real problem is."

"And what is that?"

"I think the real problem is that you have been sheltered by your father. You haven't been out in the marriage-mart, your father has forced his hand with every suitor that even looks your way, and you don't have any male friends of title to educate you on what is expected. You are a gently raised country girl who is clearly unaware of how the world works."

"I don't understand." Elizabeth shook her head in confusion. How could one problem be related to another?

"Of course you don't, dear. Your world is this cozy little cocoon your father built for you." She held out her hands, demonstrating the opulence surrounding them. "He's provided you with everything to keep you at his side-and from experiencing the world outside these walls."

"I'm not following your thinking. What does this have to do with how Wesley is treating me?

"My dear, Elizabeth, Wesley is acting like a normal male. It's you that isn't aware of how out of balance you are," Lilith continued, "you see, when a young man expresses interest in a young woman it isn't unusual for them to fraternize with each other."

Elizabeth wasn't sure she was hearing Lilith correctly. Her mind couldn't possibly wrap itself around the words coming out of her mouth. Had she suggested that they-no, it was impossible.

"I don't know what you are insinuating, Lilith, but I'm not that kind of woman," she said in a frank tone.

"Yes, well, I'm sure your future husband wouldn't expect you to remain a virgin all these years, especially at your age." Lilith took another sip of her wine as if she suggested Elizabeth change her gown instead of suggesting she commit fornication with her step-brother.

"Lilith!" Elizabeth couldn't bring herself to say the things she wished.

"All I'm saying is that if you allowed yourself the freedom that everyone else enjoys, then who is there to blame?"

Elizabeth sat in shock as she stared back at Lilith, confounded and perplexed at her step-mother's audacity. It only took a moment before a fresh insurgence of anger replaced her fear.

"Get out!" she hissed. Lilith looked at the seething Elizabeth as if she had gone insane.

"What has gotten in to you, Elizabeth? I'm just telling you how the world really is," she said in a matter-of-fact tone.

"I said get out!" This time Elizabeth stood and pointed in the direction of the door, fixing Lilith with wildly angry, hurt eyes. Complying with her wishes, Lilith stood and exited the rooms without a backward glance.

Elizabeth shook as she fell back into her seat, her legs unable to support her any longer. She covered her face with her hands and breathed in deep trying to gain control over her emotions, but it was pointless. The words had been burned into her brain. She was encouraged to sin against herself and God by sleeping with that loathsome specimen just because he expressed his interest in her? How preposterous!

She needed to get out of here. She needed to escape, but where? Was there anywhere safe for her now?

"Elizabeth, what a pleasant surprise," Lincoln said, glad that he was having a good day and able to receive her for a visit. "You look troubled."

"No, I'm all right. You, on the other hand, look like you aren't in any condition to receive visitors, if I may be so bold. How are you feeling?" she asked, noting the pallid tone of his face and cool hands.

"I'm a little tired, but I would never refuse you, Miss Elizabeth. Come and pleasure me with your company."

"Well, I came to see how your new gardener is doing. I see he has been working on the west wall vines that you always wanted to have removed."

"Yes, I think it will improve the looks. If all works well, I hope to have a fine fountain and a mural depicting an Italian waterway."

"Oh how lovely. Who will be the painter?"

"Hopefully you my dear, I was hoping you would take that commission over painting my portrait," he said with an apologetic gaze.

"Oh," Elizabeth said with a bit of disappointment in her voice, "it wasn't the act of painting I wanted to perform. I wanted to capture your likeness. I want to paint *you*."

Lincoln wasn't prepared for such an answer. The emotional appeal was seismic, rocking his grip on the tranquility he worked so hard to achieve. He sat, contemplating her request while controlling his anxiety, waiting for his heart to slow its beat. He began to sweat under the strain of the proposal.

"I can see that you are not quite up to the task. I won't press you into something that makes you feel uncomfortable." There was no reason to over-stress the man. He looked as if he wanted to run out of the room when discussing the project. Elizabeth gaged that he was not only unable to be seen out-of-doors, but disliked the notion of being seen altogether. She felt pity for her friend and resentful of the woman who made him this way.

"It isn't that I'm refusing your talents, Miss Elizabeth. I want to please you, but I feel my emotional status won't allow me to be a good subject." Lincoln wasn't aware that he was gripping the arm of the chair. Elizabeth wasn't about to let the man remain white-knuckled over her request.

"I don't think you understand, Sir Athelston, I can paint you however you want to be seen," she said.

Realization hit Lincoln like a wave on the rocks. Yes, he could tell her, have her create an alternate appearance for him. He didn't have to look like an emotionally liable and weary older man. He could appear as the confident, self-assured man he used to be. Tranquility washed over him as he pictured himself in a regal pose with his grandfather's sword and the tunic his daughter made for him, the royal blue with gold embroidery would bring out his eyes. He would have to have every detail in place to keep his composure in check.

"Can you come over again tomorrow? I should be able to give you an answer then," he said with a degree of hope that Elizabeth didn't expect.

"Yes, I will." She felt victorious a putting Sir Athelston at ease, making her smile the entire ride home.

Elizabeth entered the great room, breathing in the aroma of fresh rushes placed on the floor. First heading toward the kitchen to request refreshments, she planned on filling the day with writing her daily letter to Kathryn informing her of the great success at acquiring Sir Athelston as her next subject, after the baby arrives that is. She glanced about the room, landing her eyes on Darwin. Approaching him, Elizabeth knew by the set of his face that something was amiss. Three maids appeared out of nowhere and lined up behind her like little ducklings.

"Darwin, what is going on?" she asked.

Darwin stood stock straight, affixed his gaze on the wall behind Elizabeth and lied. "Nothing is 'going on', Miss Hollingberry." Elizabeth's eyebrows shot up. When did Darwin ever call her 'Miss Hollingberry'? Never, that's when.

She addressed him again to begin her inquisition only to stop as soon as she noticed the change in his demeanor. Wesley had entered the room. She knew it even before she saw him. Had news of his antics spread throughout the house? Of course it had. Everyone knew that servants were known gossipers, especially if their household was in jeopardy and Listhenshire definitely had trouble afoot.

"Good afternoon, Elizabeth," Wesley said with a bow. At least he had the common sense to act remorseful. He carried a sullen air about him like a shroud and looked like he hadn't slept well. All the better. He should feel guilty, for that's exactly what he was. She felt a sappy apology coming, one which she was not in any frame of mind to accept.

"Excuse me, for I have suddenly lost my appetite." Elizabeth felt her stomach turn with disgust. She couldn't bring herself to look at him, let alone return his salutation. She was followed out of the room by the three ducklings.

"Miss Elizabeth!" A hard whisper came from behind her as she exited the dining room. She turned to see who hailed her in such a manner. It was the cook, wrapped in her white apron and waving a dish cloth to get her attention.

"Yes, Martha?" Now was not the time to collaborate with the cook on this week's menu.

"Come, please." The portly woman gestured for her to come into the servant's stairwell.

"Martha, what is going on? First these three maids are at my feet every step, and then Darwin is acting strange, now you are whispering for me in concealment. What has happened?"

Martha pulled her through the kitchen by the hand without saying a word. She led Elizabeth to the servant's quarters. The dark hallway bespoke of the ominous feeling that overcame her. Something dreadful had happened. They stopped before what she knew as Charlotte's room. Chills ran down Elizabeth's spine. Martha opened the door.

"We found her at the bottom of the stairs not long ago," Martha explained while Elizabeth took in the sight before her. "We found her unconscious. No one knows when or how it happened."

Elizabeth stood frozen, her breath captured tight in her chest, her eyes welled up for her loyal servant. It was several moments before she could regain her composure.

Marybeth stood above Charlotte's supine body, bruised and battered and her head bandaged in white linen, red showing where it had bled through. Her right arm was secured close to her body with bruised, swollen fingertips resting on her chest. Her eyes remained closed.

Elizabeth watched every rise and fall of Charlotte's chest as she moved closer to the bed, consoling herself that the maid was still alive. Tears streamed down Elizabeth's face, her breaths came out ragged and barely controlled. She reached out to cover Charlotte's hand with her own but Marybeth stopped her.

"She needs her sleep," she whispered faintly.

Elizabeth sunk to her knees beside the bed. With all the strength and might she could summon, she bowed her head and prayed for Charlotte's survival. She also prayed for justice, for she knew in her heart of hearts exactly who was behind Charlotte's injuries.

Chapter 11

"*I* FOUND SOMETHING *rather disturbing," she said, clearly flustered over the new turn of events. She handed him the missive and let him decide for himself what to do.*

He controlled the urge to throw it into the fire. How could the king have done such a thing to them? Their plans were going along smoothly, now they have to work that much faster to achieve their goal, and much more secretively. There can't be a breath of guilt coming their way if they were going to succeed in getting what they want.

"What are we to do?" she asked, noting the change of color in her cohort's face. He didn't answer, but stomped off toward the watchtower, his favorite place for thinking.

Elizabeth sent a note to Sir Athelston the next day explaining the unfortunate circumstances that prevented her visiting him as planned. It saddened her though, for she truly enjoyed their visits and bringing light into such a dark, dismal place he created for himself. Regardless, she needed to help take care of Charlotte and see to her needs before she followed her heart's desire.

Before she set out to commence her day, she wrote a quick letter to Kathryn, glossing over the details of the household. She also told her of the success of acquiring her next subject before closing with her usual farewell and hopes in seeing her soon.

The house was empty, for Darwin informed her that Edward and Wesley went to conduct some business and Lilith was in her greenhouse tending to her roses she so prized. Even better news was that Charlotte had regained consciousness and was able to talk but was unable to remain awake for more than a few moments. Still, Elizabeth pressed her vigil at her bedside. She stayed until she was summoned to dine with the family.

The somber look on everyone's face was enough to make Elizabeth want to turn tail before they noticed her presence.

"Come in, my dear, we have been waiting for you." Edward motioned for her to take her seat.

"Yes, Papa," she complied with sluggishness, noting the unsmiling faces coming from the other side of the table. Deciding to carry herself with dignity and not let the mother and son pair unravel her, she sat and smiled back at them.

They were served in silence with only miniscule pleasantries passed between them. It suited Elizabeth just fine to eat in silence. There wasn't anything pleasant to speak about with Lilith or Wesley, and Edward rarely participated in banter while eating. Elizabeth found it quite enjoyable this evening, preferring to contemplate the pose in which Sir Athelston would be best suited.

"Elizabeth," Edward said solemnly, drawing everyone's attention, "I think it is time you visit Caprington Castle for a time. I have it on good authority that the last days of pregnancy are the hardest to endure. Go see Mrs. Cunninghame and come back at leisure. I'm sure she will be grateful."

Elizabeth couldn't have been more surprised. She nearly squealed in delight had she not contained her emotions, but suddenly recalled her duty here.

"But what of Charlotte?" she asked with true concern in her voice.

"Marybeth is quite capable of taking care of her daughter. There are plenty of people to help her as well. The Boulstridges aren't so fortunate. They've had to send most of their servants away for the lack of support. You'll be needed there more than here."

"Oh, thank you, Papa. I'm sure Kathryn will thank you too." Elizabeth wasted no time in packing. She wasn't sure how long she would be at Caprington, so she decided to pack the majority of her things. She was going to settle in for a nice long stay, reveling in every moment in helping her friend and the newborn. She could barely stand the excitement. She took a carpetbag full of personal belongings and made arrangements for her trunks to be delivered on the marrow.

Edward, Lilith and Wesley saw her off. She was glad to be away from home, even if it were for a short time. She felt that separating herself was the best action, allowing her to think things through with clarity, and possibly gaining a new perspective while she was away.

"Come on Wesley, we have a full day ahead." Edward was both proud of his cunning and sad at the prospect that it may not be enough to remove Elizabeth from Listhenshire. Still, he needed to do something before he lost it all.

They were to meet at the boundary line of their prospective properties, both refusing to step on the other's land for fear of being accused of trespassing, having a penalty of the offended party's choosing.

"They're late," said Edward, stating the obvious. He wasn't a very patient man. He didn't want to be here in the first place, having stated his intention to keep his property as long as the king saw fit at the last meeting. Historically, they'd sent a messenger boy who'd probably been sent to spy on the goings-on at Listhenshire. This time, all they sent was a note stating they wished to meet once more. Why, he did not know. He was quite adamant about his stand last time. Did they think he would have changed his mind in such a short time?

"How long do you think we should give them?" Wesley raised his hand to shield his eyes from the sun and looked from side to side and all around.

"None," Edward barked, "if they don't have the courtesy to attend promptly to their own meeting, then I have no obligation to stay." Edward was in no mood to meet the five Colhosters again in the first place. He directed his horse to head home and put this miserable day behind him.

"We may be early. Let's wait a little while," Wesley suggested, keeping his horse planted in its spot, "after all, we rode out here for a purpose. Let's just see what they have to say."

"They can't speak when they aren't here. Let's go. My mood is growing fouler by the second."

"Then I can help lift your mood, perhaps with a little physical activity?" Wesley jumped from his steed and pulled out his sword. "You know I'm in need of practice. My fencing coach can vouch for that." Edward stared down at Wesley, holding his sword pointed into the ground as if it were a walking stick.

"For God's sake, lad, lift up your sword with pride. If you must lower it, hold it like thus." Edward dismounted his horse and drew his sword, demonstrating the proper way to display one's weapon. "This may be fun," he concurred, "tether the horses and I'll be your pedagogue. Only for a while, though. I refuse to let those behemoths across the yard think we waited all day for them."

Edward was gentle with Wesley at first giving him verbal instruction, revisiting the rules and minor details he should have known from his instructors from university. Indeed, the boy did need to be a little more assertive, have more confidence in his moves than he was displaying. He proved to have good strength and grip, but he seemed unsure of himself wielding the thing. "I'll be sure to give you more time with your fencing master in the future," Edward declared, almost embarrassed by the lack of prowess Wesley was exhibiting. It wouldn't do to have a weakling defending what he worked so hard to build up. "Pick it up, Wesley. Show me you can defend yourself. Pretend I'm a Colhoster and fight me like a man!"

Edward pushed him harder, forcing him to protect himself, all the while telling him what he should be doing and what move he was planning next. They were engaged in swordplay for nearly an hour when Edward called for a breather. They were both winded and needed to redirect their thoughts-Edward to the task of teaching the boy, and Wesley to grasp the art of fighting.

"How long has it been since your last lesson, Wesley?" Edward said between puffs.

"It might have been a couple of years."

"A couple of years? They were supposed to be teaching you this at university! What happened?" Edward asked, having the mind to write the headmaster and demand an explanation.

"It wasn't their fault. I was more interested in academics than sword play."

"I see," Edward replied, clearly disappointed, "you'll have to pay dearly for that indiscretion. I want you to be a master swordsman by the end of the summer."

Edward reconvened the swordplay, continuing Wesley's instruction. He pushed him harder than before, daring Wesley into more vigorous fighting than he was used to participating in. It came as quite a surprise how good it felt to instruct the boy. As a father of only girls, Edward had missed out on raising sons. Then a thought occurred to him, Lilith was still young enough to bare children. He could try to conceive with her. And that thought, that little bit of distraction rattling around in his head slowed his reflexes allowing Wesley's lunge for his mark.

Edward could have sworn Wesley was aiming for his heart but pierced through his arm instead. Edward recoiled, taking in the sight of blood quickly staining his sleeve. In that moment, Edward could have sworn Wesley's faced morphed from disappointed surprise to horrified and remorseful and his words laced with concern and self-reproach.

"It's all right, son. Get me a rag and tie it about my arm. I'll live long enough to make it home." The bleeding was temporarily obstructed by the bandage, but he had nothing to interfere with the seething pain emanating from the puncture. Before mounting his horse, Edward glanced about. No sign of the Colhosters. It's just as well. Nothing would have come from the meeting anyway.

Edward's day went from bad to worse as he drew closer to Listhenshire, for he saw the army encampment inside the bailey. He'd sent Elizabeth off just in time, he thought. Enshrouding himself with an air of bravado, Edward strode into the castle prepared to lie through his teeth.

Chapter 12

"**S**HE RAN AWAY?" Gabriel parroted Lord Hollingberry. He wanted to run away himself, for that matter, but he was here in edict of the king and was prepared to see it fulfilled. He wasn't about to show cowardice as this woman chose to do.

"Yes, she thought of marriage as so distasteful that she ran off. You can check her rooms to verify for yourself that she took all her belongings." With his chest distended and nose in the air, Edward was proud of thwarting the king's plan without seeming unlawful.

"Do you know where she would go?" Gabriel asked, knowing full well that Edward Hollingberry was going to lie to him. He looked away and placed his hands behind his back to hide his nervousness.

"No, Lord Athelston, I do not. She slipped out with nary a word and I suppose she wanted it that way."

"Yes, I suppose she would. Tell me, Lord Hollingberry, how does one 'slip out' with her entire wardrobe and belongings?" Gabriel nailed Edward with a hard look. The man stammered in effort to think quickly of a reply.

"She left while we, my wife and I, were away. The servants told us that she left unattended."

"What was she traveling in? Obviously she would need a coach and driver. She couldn't very well take all of her belongings in her arms astride a horse, now could she?" he pressed, enjoying the pursuit of the truth.

"I don't believe any of our drivers took her to her destination. Perhaps she had assistance from a friend," he blubbered, yearning for a drink at this moment.

"Perhaps," Gabriel didn't believe a word the man said. "How did you become injured?"

"My step-son and I were practicing our sword fighting. He needs a little more practice."

"Now that is something I can believe." Gabriel noted the young man standing in the back of the room milling about the rushes. There was no point in putting any more questions to the lying man. He would have to search for her himself. It was bad enough to be tethered to the chit, now he had to expend time and energy, both of which were running low, to find her and make her comply with the same mandate he was held to. It made him all that much more resentful of the situation.

Good fortune met him at the door in the form of a flat wagon with trunks upon it as he entered the baily. Having just embarked toward its destination, he mounted his horse for the hunt.

"Where are you off to?" Bernard asked, noting the intent look in his commander's eyes.

"Off to find my wife," Gabriel said as he pointed to the wagon full of someone's belongings. "Come, this may be fun." The two followed at a discrete distance until it stopped in front of a castle fifteen miles away from Listhenshire. "This is Caprington Castle. If my memory serves me correctly, it is owned by the Boulstridge family. If we are lucky, I know someone that will be of assistance."

Caleb Cunninghame greeted his long-lost friend Gabriel with a firm handshake and an introduction to Bernard Cabrara. They were invited in for ale before getting down to business, but Gabriel wanted to be finished with this.

"My friend, I didn't come for a social visit. I've come to collect my reluctant bride," he stated.

"Good for you, my man," he said with a manly clap to his friend's arm. "I was wondering who you would have chosen. Is she from court?"

"No, and she wasn't of my choosing," Gabriel ground out. "If it were up to me I would remain single. I'm under edict from the king, therefore, I am obliged to be married."

"I understand and I offer my condolences to the bride," Caleb quipped, knowing what a hard row this woman would have married to someone with the likes of Gabriel Athelston, especially when he was forced to do something he didn't want to do. "So, will you tell me who this unfortunate lady is?"

"Miss Elizabeth Hollingberry," Gabriel announced.

Caleb was rocked with shock and dismay. He viewed Elizabeth as someone who would invite a husband, not withdraw from one. He was also disappointed that her plight wasn't mentioned when she arrived.

"I think you are mistaken, Gabriel, she arrived just last night to help my wife birth our child. She didn't seem like one that was running away."

"Women are cunning, Caleb, and this one seems to be no different." Gabriel's resolve was evident and Caleb didn't have any other recourse than to produce Elizabeth and get straight to the matter.

"Please fetch Miss Hollingberry," Caleb commanded a servant.

"That would be poor timing, Sir. Your wife has gone into labor and I would be hard pressed to tear her away," the old man stated, disinterested in entering that arena in any case.

Caleb rushed up to his wife's birthing bed as fast as his legs could carry him, instantly forgetting the guests in his great room. He waited on the opposite side of the door for hours listening to the grunts and screams coming from his wife. As soon as it was over, though, he entered to find a beautiful baby boy being cared for by the nurse and Elizabeth cleaning herself up. Caleb laid beside his wife and crooned loving words into her ear, praising her for giving him such a beautiful boy.

Elizabeth slipped out the door, leaving the two to glow over their new son. She was covered in blood and desperately needed to change. Knowing there were minimal servants about, she headed to the kitchen to fetch some water.

She navigated the stairs with ease, a smile gracing her face from the blessing of ushering in a new life. She was so lost in the reverie of her happiness that she nearly ran into a soldier in the hallway. Expressing her apologies, she continued to the kitchen.

Gabriel had grown tired of waiting for this illusive chit. He was not going to wait around like a sap, letting her run from him and then make him wait. For all he knew, this was a ruse to give her time to get away yet again. He was in no mood to be anyone's pawn to move about as they see fit. He stalked off looking in each room, growing more irate with each empty room. The sheer lack of staffing only amplified his irritation. The last place to check on the first level was the rectory before he worked his way upstairs.

The rectory door closed with a loud thump as he propelled himself toward the stairwell, only to be brought up short by the woman descending the stairs with a contentedly happy look about her. The tell-tale stains of blood on her clothing revealed that she truly was involved in the birthing of a child, but the staining of her garments did nothing to detract from the comeliness of her face.

Her soft features were complementary to her soft, large round eyes with the longest eyelashes he'd ever seen. Her soft pink lips were curved into a smile that reached her lovely eyes, conveying contentedness and satisfaction. He followed her into the kitchen as if drawn into her wake, not resisting its pull. She hadn't realized he was standing behind her when she removed her apron and placed it in cool water to soak then removed the tent-like smock that protected her clothing.

Gabriel was pleasantly surprised by the slim figure he saw before him, momentarily forgetting that he was an unwilling participant in this forced marriage. She was fashionably dressed but he could tell that she wasn't wearing a corset, which only fueled his imagination.

Elizabeth continued washing the blood out of the white apron as best she could unaware of the man behind her. A tune popped into her head and she began to hum, gleefully purring each note as she worked. After she was satisfied with her work, she rung out the apron and placed it on the small rope beside the oven before unrolling her sleeves.

When she turned around, she was so startled that she almost fell to her knees in freight. She caught herself against the sink and righted herself. A tall man with dark hair, bright blue eyes and ruggedly handsome features stood silently dressed from head to toe in king's mail. His dark colored tunic brought out his tanned skin and the large coat of arms hanging from a thick chain around his neck projected his importance. This was a man of the king, there was no doubt in her mind. It was puzzling, though, when his expression went from sultry to disdain.

"I'm sorry if I startled you, but I didn't want to give you the opportunity to run away again," he said with contempt.

"I beg your pardon, sir. You must have me confused with someone else. I don't believe we've met. My name is Elizabeth Hollingberry." She flashed her green eyes at him in her beguiling way.

"Yes, I know who you are. I am Gabriel Athelston of Laughtonwood," he said, gaging her reaction. He was surprised when it didn't illicit the expected response.

"Oh yes. You are Sir Lincoln's son. He's talked about you often." Elizabeth's unease relaxed and she smiled at him, prompting a peculiar look from the man.

"I'm also your husband," he said with one brow cocked.

"I don't think so. I'm sure I would remember such a thing." Elizabeth's heart raced with his words, becoming fearful of this stranger, wondering if this man was making up some story before accosting her. She began to inch away from him.

Gabriel saw the denial then fear cross her beautiful face. She truly hadn't known, now she was afraid of him. His mind went back to the meeting with her father and knew the source of the deception.

"Don't be afraid, Miss Hollingberry. I have an edict from the king." He reached into his tunic and pulled out a document with the king's seal clearly visible. She stayed in place, determining whether she should trust him. Reading her mind, Gabriel placed it on the table and slid it over to her.

To his relief, she took the document and read it aloud. He was impressed with her ability to read at all, let alone with the proficiency in which she displayed. Her breathing increased with the impact of realization. She absently sat in the nearest chair as her mind raced.

"What will my father say when he finds out?" she asked.

"He already knows and has known for some time," Gabriel said bluntly, taking a seat across from her.

"How can you say that when I didn't even know?" she accused.

"The king's secretary wrote to him weeks ago. I also talked with him earlier today. He said you ran away in effort to elude marriage."

Elizabeth gasped in surprise, stopping herself from calling this man a liar. Biting her tongue and taking a deep breath, she forced herself to think. She couldn't fathom her father intervening in such a way. It was fortunate for Kathryn that she was sent early, but as she thought harder, things began falling into place.

"That would explain his recent behavior. I don't think he was doing it out of maliciousness. I hope you forgive him for the love of his daughter." Elizabeth was reassured by his return nod, solemn as it was. Looking down at the edict once more, she resigned herself to reality as it was presented. "Married?"

Gabriel heard a fair amount of uncertainty in her voice, taking it as nervousness at embarking on the new and sudden change. He stood and rounded the table, extending his hand. She accepted it and stood with him. He bent over her hand and kissed the back letting his eyes convey his desire for her.

"Married," he repeated definitively, finding his reluctance to comply wane.

Chapter 13

"**H**E'S HERE AND *he's got her. He went out after her. For certain our plan will fail,*" she said, *fretting from the strain of it all.*

"*Don't worry I'll come up with something.*" He hated change, especially when it brought with it women who whined and fretted at every little thing.

"*But what?*" she was beside herself, unable to control her fear.

"*Get a hold of yourself woman! If you don't control yourself, you'll be out of it!*"

"*No, you wouldn't!*" She could feel herself perspire at his threat.

"*Then pipe down and don't hound me. I'll come up with something. We'll have to be more cunning, but it can still be done.*" As he strode out of the room to place as much space between them as quickly as possible, a thought occurred to him. He had an opportunity that he wouldn't otherwise have if Elizabeth hadn't been sent away. His imagination ran with possibilities. His steps quickened with his heart beat for the exhilaration coursing through his veins.

"Caleb speaks highly of you." Elizabeth said as a means to strike up conversation over the intimate dinner she was sharing with her new husband.

"I would do the same for him. We met at court many years ago. He was the chief architect working on a pet project of the king when I met him. He wasn't yet married to Kathryn." Gabriel was at ease talking with Elizabeth, enjoying their meager meal of kippers and cabbage despite the taste.

"As you might have guessed, Kathryn and I have been friends since birth. I had a hard time adjusting to life without her after she married. Now, it seems like there are other adjustments on the horizon," she said, having been told that they would be leaving for the Scottish-English border after the marriage ceremony.

"You'll like Piffenview. It's beautiful this time of year."

"I'm sure I will. I'm looking forward to exploring the landscape with Majesty," she said. "That is my horse. I named her after the king. She is very regal and so needed a name that suited. Do you think it is too disrespectful?" she asked.

"No, I don't. Do you ride often?" Both of them had abandoned their plates for the much more pleasant interaction.

"As often as I can. Do you have plans to see your father in your brief stay?" she asked, hitting a nerve she hadn't been aware was raw and tender. His jaw tightened and his smile disappeared. "I see, well, I'm on good terms with him and am positive he will be pleasantly surprised to hear that I will be becoming part of the family."

"No doubt," he said, wanting to get off this subject as fast as possible. "Caleb has asked if you could stay on for just a little while longer," he said.

"May I?" she asked with her heart in her throat. Gabriel delayed answering her, giving her a pondering stare.

Elizabeth looked up with intense interest to his answer, not only giving Kathryn much needed support with the baby but to spend a few extra precious moments with her best friend. Her searching eyes were upon him, not letting anything escape her notice.

"Yes, you may," he said before abruptly leaving the table and the kitchen, leaving Elizabeth wondering what she did wrong.

Gabriel wished he hadn't sent Bernard away so soon after securing Elizabeth's compliance. He could use a sparring partner right now, feeling the need to strike something. He'd forgotten how quickly women turned conniving and duplicitous using any ploy at their disposal to get what they want and Elizabeth was no different. He saw it in her eyes, the way she worked her lashes, batting them while flashing her needful eyes at him. He couldn't believe he'd fallen for her innocent demeanor and coy trickeries. How dare she act subservient, playing the submissive card so early in the game showed him just how much of a fool he'd been to be drawn so easily by her beauty. He bid a brief farewell to Caleb with well-wishes to his wife and their new son before heading back to Listhenshire.

"Two days? You want to exchange nuptials and be off, just like that?" Edward said, snapping his fingers.

"I want to relieve Lord Garrott from his post as soon as possible, seeing that his health is failing. I see no reason to tarry." Gabriel stood soldier straight without looking at Edward, not giving him the chance to make an emotional plea. He was confident he could have Sir Otholomew's investigation wrapped up by then, allowing him the advantage of a quick departure.

"A proper wedding needs time. She has sisters that will want to travel from far away for such an event. Lords and ladies from across the countryside will want to attend, which will overtax the dressmakers if they have less than a month to work with," Edward argued, only receiving silence from the stone-faced man, his soon to be son-in-law. "Did you speak of this to Elizabeth? Oh, never mind, I know the answer she would give. By now she already sees you as her husband."

"I am, by law, her husband. The ceremony is only a ritual. In the kings eyes we are already husband and wife." Gabriel broke his stoic stare to observe the white-haired man with a growing paunch. Nothing had changed. The anxiety was there in his eyes, the tenseness remained in his shoulders and his hands were still clenched in a perpetual state of wringing.

"If we could reach some sort of agreement, perhaps even securing your post with your men then coming back for her. The wedding will be planned and all will be present upon your return. That would work out splendidly." Edward smiled nervously, hoping against hope that Gabriel would agree.

"No. I am not in a position to do such a thing," Gabriel said.

"Then we will schedule it for thirty days henceforth. That will give us time to do all that is needed."

"One week is more than enough time to gather witnesses from the community." Gabriel was in no mood to linger here. Edward started and stuttered at the man's audacity.

"Barely! Three weeks is the utter minimum needed."

"Then you have two weeks," Gabriel abruptly turned and walked away, ending any argument Edward would have made.

"Have you agreed on a name?" Elizabeth smiled as she held the beautiful baby boy while his mother adjusted her clothing after feeding him.

"No, we haven't even talked about it. There is still time. I'd like to think it over before giving him something that he will be stuck with for the rest of his life. I'd like to see his personality first," Kathryn said, reaching for the tray of fruit, cheese and bread at her bedside. "Nursing makes me so hungry."

"Ma'am, your trunks have been placed in the suite next door with your instructions to leave them packed, but this was something that I thought you might want now." The maid brought forth the small tin for her. "It has sweeties inside. I was afraid they may go stale before you reached your new destination."

"Thank you, you can put them on the table for now," Elizabeth said.

"Oh, may I have one? I find myself afflicted with a sweet tooth right about now."

"Of course you may, Kathryn. Help yourself because I have the sweetest thing here in my arms."

"Let me see, I think I will choose the lemon with powdered sugar." Kathryn reached in and took a bite of the pastry, instantly cringing. "I think your cook was a little heavy with the sugar, Elizabeth. It's sickeningly sweet."

"Let me try," she said, opening her mouth for Kathryn to pop the other half into her mouth without letting loose of the precious child.

"You're right, it almost drowns out the lemon. Do you want to try another and see if it is the same?" she asked.

"No, the last one is upsetting my stomach." Kathryn laid back with a furrowed brow.

"Ouch!" Elizabeth involuntarily yelped and doubled over while holding onto the babe. "My stomach is cramping," she said, barely making it to the cradle before everything in her stomach revolted and violently ejected. She could hear Kathryn suffering with the same malady.

She knew then that they'd been poisoned. It seemed that her future father-in-law as wrong, for the bandits creating so much havoc with the neighbors had indeed progressed to mortal crimes. Her last thought was of Gabriel and that she would never know what it was like to be truly married.

"They were found unconscious, my lord, with the poison sitting beside them," the manservant said with a tear-stricken face.

"Have you tested it to be sure?" Gabriel tried to keep his emotions intact while finding the culprit, feeling the intense urge to strike something.

"No, my lord, but it is the most likely source. A maid had found the treats in Elizabeth's trunks and delivered them to her just before they were stricken. She is most certainly shattered for her part in causing Mrs. Cunninghame and Miss Hollingberry harm. They are both beloved."

Gabriel was escorted up to the room where both women were being taken care of in the same bed out of convenience. Their sallow skin and glazed eyes made Gabriel's blood boil. He immediately turned on his heel determined to find who had done this.

With Bernard, Gabriel's personal physician, taking control of treating the women, Gabriel's first task was completed within moments, confirming the tarts were indeed poisoned. The small amount he'd given to the rabbit he'd taken from the kitchen's pens worked fast and brutally, not sparing its life as it had the women. Next, he questioned the maid who could barely control herself, but was able to tell him that the tin was inside the larger trunk on top of the clothes. There was no note, no labeling, not even a ribbon tied about it.

"Pecor, Wiggins," Gabriel called out to the only other two men traveling with him, "I want all foodstuffs from Caprington as well as Listhenshire confiscated and tested. I want to know who did this and why."

"Do you think this is the doing of her father in order to keep her from you?" Wiggins asked.

"No, but I will be investigating that notion. Bring the family here. Let me question them outside of the security of their own home. Meanwhile, share our provisions with the households." Gabriel dismissed his men and went on a search himself.

Chapter 14

"I DON'T KNOW what could have been used to kill our garden so quickly and so thoroughly," Mr. Lowsley said, perplexed to this day how someone could be so vicious as to destroy a lovely garden such as his. He stared upon the brown, shriveled grass and all the greenery that now stood charred and blackened but wholly intact, standing in direct contrast with the rest of the garden still teaming with life.

"Can you speculate who would do this, or at least have access to chemicals that could do this?" Gabriel asked the distraught man.

"No not at present. I don't even know what kind of chemical would do such damage." Mr. Lowsley turned away from the hideous sight with the disparaging words of his gardener echoing through his thoughts. There won't be any planting for many years. This parcel of land is dead to the core.

Gabriel had his thoughts, but wisely kept them to himself. He wondered if the poison that killed the Lowsley's foliage was the same that poisoned Elizabeth and Kathryn. From Sir Otholomew's viewpoint, the incidents in this community were anonymous and depersonalized by striking things far removed from people. This was an acute and severe turn from mere hoodlum vandalism. Sir Otholomew had misjudged whoever it was causing such destruction.

The course of his investigation lead him to the Hessencastle residence where the charred remains of the servants' housing unit stood in homage to the destructive power of this rogue villain with its owner standing before it as irate now as he was the day it happened.

"I can't explain it. There were no servants inside, or even near it for that matter, so there were no witness. It is quite unexplainable," Sir Hessencastle said.

"It looks like the blaze started from here. Was there an explosion of some sort?" Gabriel pried and peeled within the rubble to determine the true cause.

"I'm not aware of any explosion, Lord Athelston. I saw flames from a distance and by the time we drew near, the structure was a total loss."

"Then why do you think that it was anything more than an unfortunate incident?"

"Because it happened after Sir Lowsley's garden was ruined and the Colhoster's forge mill was demolished," he said with certainty and conviction in his voice.

"I believe you are correct, Sir Hessencastle," Gabriel said, presenting what he knew was the cause of the fire.

"What is it?" Sir Hessencastle asked as he peered at the chunk of distorted metal.

"It is, or was, a small box that held a combustible material. The fact that you didn't hear the explosion tells me that the person didn't use very much, allowing him to start the blaze and disappear undetected. Do you see this line of charred grass? If you follow it you will see that it leads behind a hedge. That is where he lit the fuse that traveled straight to the box filled with this explosive material, allowing him a clean get-away as well as to protect himself from getting hurt."

"I don't recall seeing that line before. How did I miss such a clue?" he asked rather flabbergasted.

"It is the effects of living in the country, I suppose. You aren't used to such villainy. I'm going to investigate the forge mill explosion where I suspect I will find the same clue," he said, placing the contorted metal box in the purse tied to his saddle.

"God speed Lord Athelston. We need to find this hoodlum before it is too late," Sir Hessencastle said, knowing this could only end badly if allowed to continue. "Here come two of your men to help you."

Gabriel saw them before Sir Hessencastle and knew that they were not riding to assist, but riding in urgency. He mounted and met them a good distance away from Sir Hessencastle's ears, for he didn't want to distress the man any more than he already was. His gut was telling him that he was not going to like any news brought to him.

"There has been a development. Come quickly. There is no time to explain," Pecor said breathlessly.

Indeed, there was much trouble afoot and escalating with time. Gabriel saw the eminent threat sitting just inside the forest surrounding Caprington Castle. He was told that the Colhoster clan had moved quickly and swiftly after word had spread that the Boulstridge family was closely targeted by the anonymous criminal.

"It is worse than it seems, sir. This morning, soon after you left Listhenshire, a discovery of dead rabbits was found. They were the family's food source, not wild hare. They were caged, yet all are dead," Pecor said.

"How long between this discovery and the arrival of the Colhosters?" he asked forebodingly.

"Within hours," he replied, making his own assumption of the situation.

Without a word, Gabriel turned on his heal and headed for Listhenshire to fetch reinforcements. He wasn't about to let this carry on any further and was determined to finished it quickly.

The house was empty, save for a few servants. The rabbits were left untouched, much to Gabriel's relief. A fine white powder dusted each of the rabbits' food bowls. There was no doubt that this same powder was the same causing all the misery, destruction and mayhem in this small, quiet countryside.

Caprington Castle was not under siege just yet, but by the looks of the bailey, the inner courtyard, and the chaos running amok within the castle walls bespoke otherwise. Gabriel knew that Caleb Cunninghame was standing in as head of the Boulstridge household and was thoroughly disappointed at the leadership, or the lack thereof, Caleb was exercising at this moment.

Gabriel understood Caleb's need to see after his wife and new child, but the eminent threat was higher priority in any case. They must stand and fight if they're to keep what they have and he was compelled to tell him so.

Gabriel's impatience impelled him to go in search for his friend, only to be directed to the rectory. He entered fueled with righteous indignation at the insensibility of Caleb's inactivity but was brought him up short at the sight of Caleb comforting Rose Boulstridge, Kathryn's aunt, before a covered body. Gabriel's impatience immediately deflated.

Not knowing how long the two were intending to remain kneeling before their deceased loved one, Gabriel decided to make his presence known by discreetly clearing his throat.

"Gabriel! I'm very thankful, to see you. We could use your help right about now."

"What happened?" Gabriel feared the worst.

"Kathryn's mother was very ill, but after learning about the goings-on and knowing that her home was threatened, she couldn't take the stress of the unknown and the visible threat of her home being overtaken. She suffered an apoplexy and died. We tried to keep her ignorant of such things, but there was no way to keep it from her." Caleb guided the distraught Rose into the corridor, letting her lady's maid escort her to her rooms then turned back to his friend, utterly spent with emotion.

"We must talk, my friend," Gabriel said, clasping Caleb's shoulder in a reassuring grip.

"I've made a mess of things, I know. You must think me inept, but in my defense, Iris didn't have enough resources to properly defend her towers. I had fully intended to rectify the situation, but a few days wasn't enough time to fulfill that need."

"There is no explanation needed, Caleb. You have the king's army at your disposal. We need to talk about the attacks that have been happening."

"I don't know how much assistance I can be. We have only been here for several weeks, not enough time to do any investigation of my own. As of now, I'm preoccupied with seeing after my wife's recovery. I feel inadequate to help either of our wives, let alone pretend to know what has caused this."

"They were poisoned with arsenic." Gabriel let it sink in to Caleb's painful reverie. "Kathryn and Elizabeth were not the only ones who experienced the effects of this poison. Every incident surrounding you gives evidence that arsenic is to blame."

"How can that be?" Caleb asked, unfamiliar with the substance.

"It is not only poisonous, but it is also volatile when heated. It was used to kill vegetation, ignite a fire and create an explosion. Unfortunately, the antics have escalated to human involvement. What activity has your enemy been making?" he asked, eager to confront the offending clan.

"Nothing as of yet," Caleb said with the strain of his cumulative worries beginning to show on his face. "I have to admit that, before your arrival, it felt like doom."

Gabriel knew that, regardless of who was the head of household here, he would have to intervene. He wasn't about to let land-hungry murderers get away from running about the king's countryside unchecked. "Don't worry, my friend. You have a defense now."

Gabriel set his men into motion. He divided his forces equally, bringing two thousand men to Caprington with him. They were all instructed to keep close watch over all foodstuffs and not to drink the water. Several covert groups were sent to fetch water from upstream of the offending clan. All stored goods in the household were strictly off limits.

Knowing that the Colhosters could sit outside the walls for weeks without a word or action, Gabriel decided to force their hand. If the Colhosters thought they were going to have an easy acquisition, they were in for a big surprise.

As directed, Edward Hollingberry brought his young wife, Lilith, and her son, Wesley, with him to see to Elizabeth's condition after hearing of the attack. Lilith's emotions overcame her and Edward guided her to sit on the couch beside him, consoling her as she sobbed. The attractive blonde was clearly distraught as she contemplated the situation.

"I knew those barbarians were up to no good. I never did trust them," the woman cried into Edward's shoulder. "Now that they've harmed our Elizabeth there is no doubt in my mind that they should pay."

"What are their demands?" Edward growled, barely controlling his rage, wanting to mete out justice swiftly.

"They haven't made any. It won't be long before they approach. I suspect they're gathering their wits not having expected a good portion of the king's military force to arrive as we did."

"And with all your military might," the boy vented, "why don't you go out and slay every last one after all they've done? They should be eradicated from the face of this earth," Wesley spat with all the malediction he could contrive.

Gabriel was taken aback by the vehement exclamation by the young boy. He'd nearly spat his malcontent of Gabriel's inaction then promptly returned to the introverted, thumbnail chewing state he'd previously been.

"I cannot, in good conscience, take action without first allowing the offending party to surrender their position and retreat. If they pursue their stance and decide to make war, they will decidedly be outnumbered by even half my men and out skilled by a quarter. Even if they choose to acquiesce, they will not go unpunished. I will see to it that the king hears of their actions and they pay dearly for it."

"So we just sit here and wait? We're sitting ducks!" Lilith was showing signs of becoming hysterical. Edward attempted to calm his wife to no avail. "How can you calmly stand before us and not wonder how they will strike next? What if they use poison again? What if they sneak through your guards in the middle of the night and kill us all? What if-"

"Lady Hollingberry, I assure you that will never happen. We've also taken measures that poisoning will not happen again. With the myriads of tactics possible, I assure you, we've prepared ourselves against them."

"But how can you be sure?" she asked, blatantly unsure of his talents.

Gabriel didn't take umbrage to the grieving woman's words as insolence, but as someone insecure with the unknown. Gabriel dealt with threats of this sort on a daily basis, but to someone who had never dealt with opposition of this nature, it would be exceedingly frightening.

"Lady Hollingberry," Gabriel knelt before the weeping woman, taking hold of a free hand, "I am a guard to the king, someone who is entrusted with his personal safety and that of the throne. The men that surround both this castle and yours are equally trained to protect the king and all that is in his interest and he has sent thousands of them with me. Have no fear of your family's safety. You couldn't be safer if you were standing in the midst of his Majesty himself." Gabriel's provision of reassurance and ample proof of his abilities, as well as the men in his command seemed to have its desired effect. Lilith stifled her tears, shoring her emotions with a visible shutter and an audible sigh. Her blue eyes blinked, bringing forth a calm exterior.

"Thank you," she replied before requesting her husband take her to their rooms so she could rest. Edward ushered her out the door and down the hallway before Wesley decided to join them, but not without first lending Gabriel a look that bespoke of his uncertainty of the situation.

"Sir, she woke," Bernard stated quietly as soon as the family left the room. Reacting instantaneously, Gabriel climbed the stairs three at a time to get to Elizabeth, only to find her quietly slumbering amidst the pile of pillows and blankets. Bernard followed as fast as he could, having a shorter stride than Gabriel's. He needed to question her, calmly interrogate her of the poisoned tarts that were found in her trunks. As he stood over her, frustration and disappointment played inside him, but not for the reason of his thwarted investigation. He found his desire to engage her again was greater than his desire to find answers. He told himself that it was merely lust that made him wish for it, to wish for her eyes to open and behold him once more.

"What happened?" he could barely push the words past his throat where a lump of emotion took up residence.

"She asked after Kathryn. She reacted to your name, but she couldn't help but fall back to sleep." The two men stood over her, staring, willing her to spontaneously wake up and reassure them of her wellbeing.

Chapter 15

E LIZABETH TEETERED ON the brink of consciousness. Still drugged
from sleep, she floated on a motionless sea of nothingness, she drifted
for miles without going anywhere. Slowly, her senses came to her. She felt
the warmth of the blankets, heard the crackle of the burning wood, tasted
the same metallic taste she recalled the last time she woke. She inhaled
and released it slowly before opening her eyes to be reminded that she
had been moved out of Kathryn's room when her vomiting abated. The
quiet crackling of the fire was interrupted with the distinct sound of a man
snoring.

Thinking that the gentleman that was treating her and Kathryn,
whose name she couldn't recall, was stationed beside her bed, she looked
over, closed her eyes in an attempt to adjust her sight in case it had failed
her, and stared, wide eyed, at someone suspiciously favoring her newly
acquired husband.

His hair was released from its cue, showing off wavy locks of black
hair. He apparently hadn't shaved in the last few days, having a manly
shadowing growing about his face. As he slept, she took in the sight of his
broad shoulders lifting with each breath, with one thick arm extended out
toward her. He had pulled the chair flush with the bed, enabling him to be
in physical contact with her.

He held her hand delicately as she slept. Her hand was dwarfed by
his as it lay on his upturned palm. Unable to withhold her emotion, a tear
appeared as she reconsidered the man who was now her husband. The

show of his tenderness without really knowing her spoke well of his true personality and drew her heart closer to him.

She traced his hand, his fingers naturally bent in relaxed slumber, his palm with the deep lines and thick calluses, his inner wrist that bespoke of a strong heart. It was an utterly beautiful, capable hand, a hand an artist could appreciate. She could see his gentle yet strong, perfectly poised in slumber as a sculpture in stone, or better yet-marble.

Placing her palm on his, gripping his thumb by the base and turning his heavy hand over, it enveloped hers. The movement woke Gabriel, instantly realizing who was doing the involuntary motion of his hand, he lifted his head to see her smiling at him, her heart in her eyes, a tear coasting its way down her cheek. Gabriel reached up and intercepted it.

"How are you feeling?" Out of the myriads of things he wanted to ask her, nothing seemed to come to mind. He gazed into her eyes and instantly forgot every blasted thing in his head.

"My stomach burns." Her hand was always placed just below her rib cage, even as she slept, as a self-soothing measure. "I feel weak, like I've been climbing a mountain for days without rest. What happened?"

"I cannot be certain, but one theory is that the vandal of Suffolk may have escalated his practices in order to gain evacuation of its inhabitance. The Colhosters have surrounded Caprington. Little is known of their intent since they have not made their stand." He watched as her mind tried to process the information, emotion rolling across her face.

"Earlier, I was told Kathryn and her son were uninjured. Is that so?"

"Yes, Kathryn is recovering in similar speed as yourself. The babe has a wet nurse and is thriving. You did not injure him when you were first afflicted," Gabriel commended, loathe to tell her of her friend's mother, but was resolved to answer her question truthfully. "Iris died after hearing of the poisonings and other strikes near to home. When the Colhosters surrounded Caprington, it was too much strain for her to bear."

Elizabeth lay astounded. She wished her mind weren't so foggy. She could feel the darkness wanting to claim her once more. She fought against it. There was something missing, some piece of information that didn't fit. She couldn't sort it out within the clutter of her thoughts. Poor Iris, there was no way of telling how horrifying a feeling like that was. Your home threatened, your children poisoned. Revelation cut in through the fog of her thoughts.

"It's my fault," she said as the fog began to lift. Realization slammed into her thoughts without buffer. A bitter moan escaped her mouth as her stomach lurched from the utter sickness that she felt over her involvement in all this. Tears sprang to her eyes in bitter reaction to the desolation she laid at another's door. Unchecked sobs bubbled forth, unable to be controlled. Emotion took over her fatigued body and mind.

This was all too much. She had to do something to stop this madness. The darkness crept upon her, stealing her thoughts from her. It would have to be another day, a stronger day, when she could tell her story. Today, she needed to sleep.

Gabriel was left alone with his thoughts, trying to decipher the meaning of the sleeping girl's statement. Pointless to wait around for several more hours until she woke once more, he immersed himself in thwarting an attack over a makeshift table with three other men when Wesley approached him.

"Lord Athelston," he called out, attempting to make his voice sound deeper and more commanding than it actually was, a force to be reckoned with and in full control of himself. His posturing gained him a raised eyebrow from Gabriel.

"Please, Wesley. We're family. Please call me Gabriel."

"Yes, of course. Gabriel, I'd like to offer my services." The four men looked at each other, disguising their true thoughts of the boy's offer. "Even if it's on the front lines, I'd like to be of use however you see fit," he said with as much courage as he could muster.

Gabriel was taken aback by the offer the boy was making to sacrifice himself for the sake of his family, and that was an admirable attribute. Unfortunately, he also saw his slight build and fair skin, noting spindly arms and legs as well as an immature presence. No, a good soldier he would not make, at least not now. After a couple more years of growing and filling out from working with a heavy sword to build his upper body strength he may be useful, but not now.

"I'm sorry, but I can't use you in the front lines right now. I have plenty of men who are well equipped to fill that need." Gabriel contemplated on how best to use the boy. "What I do need is someone to sit with Elizabeth. I would like someone there with her when she wakes."

"With all due respect, Gabriel, I feel there is a better use for me than 'woman's work'," Wesley retorted, "I'd be much more useful helping you solve this riddle than sitting beside a sleeping girl." Wesley tried his hardest to keep the disappointment off his face. *Sit with Elizabeth? How demeaning!*

"I guarantee you, Wesley, guarding a prized possession is in no way 'women's work'. Do you think a mere woman can physically defend herself against an armed man, let alone someone wholly incapable of even lifting herself out of bed?" Gabriel replied, rising from his seat and drawing a fist. He'd replied with more emotion than he'd originally intended. He calmed and reclaimed his seat. "I beg you to reconsider priority and your own station, young sir."

"My station?" Wesley questioned, thinking Gabriel was preserving him from the scene of reality, "I have studied the ways of men. I grew up on tales of how horrid man can be. My mother can tell you how we lived through attack after attack from Boarder Reivers. My father was killed while off fighting France. We had no one to protect us. Don't try to shield me, sir. It's too late for that."

"I wasn't inferring that you are gently raised, Wesley. Boys of your station are not physically groomed for the rigors of fighting. I have an army of four thousand strong, able bodied men at my command who are trained to handle the stress of war. Can you claim the same boast? Most likely your hands are as soft as your arms are weak."

"I may be young and lacking in stature, but I make up any deficiency with zeal and perseverance." Wesley's determination shone in his eyes despite the insults. "Besides, if I'm with you I will be far away from the thick of battle."

"I think not, Wesley. You misunderstand. If the Colhosters are to blame for this catastrophe, I will be the first to strike! Zeal and perseverance without knowledge and strength will get you killed. Stay here with your sister."

"But, sir-"

"Enough! I will not argue with you, Wesley. You asked how you could be of service and I told you. My decision is final." Gabriel turned his attention back to his men of confidence. "Besides, your mother will have my hide if I let anything happen to you."

Wesley stood still absorbing everything that was said. There was no swaying Gabriel. His chest began feeling tight as he thought of his prospects. He had to take another tack. He had to make sure his future and the future of his mother was secure. There must be another way.

Wesley left Gabriel and his men without another word. With internal pressures building and his imagination running rampant, Wesley felt his self-control crack. Finally, it was his mother's voice running pervasively through his mind that made him react, "Stop it!" he shouted to himself as he closed the door to his rooms. "I'll think of something," he promised himself, "I'll think of something."

"Go on Pecor. What did you find?" Justin Pecor, a man not much older than Wesley, was as cunning and perceptive as he was skilled with a blade. Having entered the service of the king at the same age Gabriel had, Justin showed promise as a good soldier, a good leader.

"It may be unrelated, but in our search of north Suffolk, Wiggins and I didn't find a cache of mutilated animals as you'd hoped. Instead, we found a badly decomposed body. The man was, most likely, astride since there were no civilized stops in the area. He also had an arrow through his neck at this angle," he said, holding a stick in a downward angle and watched Gabriel's countenance change.

"Someone laid in wait for him. It was an assassination."

"That's what we concluded and supported when we found the assassin's perch, but there haven't been any reports of missing men in these parts. He may have been a gentleman traveling alone, but there were no identifiers on him. The most we can do is lay him out and ask others to try and identify him," Pecor suggested.

"In your estimation, how long ago had he been killed?" Gabriel asked.

"My best guess would be more than a fortnight, but less than a month. We've taken the liberty to have the remains laid out with Lady Boulstridge. The family is being notified as we speak," Pecor informed.

As soon as he was able, Gabriel went to pay his respects to the dead as well as make his own examination of the man found in the woods. Unfortunately, Rose witnessed him disturbing the body, a finding that nearly brought her to her knees.

"His name was Philip," Rose said from behind her kerchief. She looked thoroughly spent from emotion, unable to bring forth another tear but still wracked with grief. Her next statement brought Gabriel to understand why. "He was my brother."

"Why wasn't he reported missing?" Gabriel asked as non-accusatory as possible.

"He wasn't due back from his mission for some time, we thought. He must have returned early," she said, not seeming to take offense. "He had investitures in the West Indies and said he would return next month.

"Do you know of anyone who may have wanted to kill him? Did he have any enemies?" Gabriel asked, surmising the sequence of events and plotting them with a newly forming theory.

"No not to my knowledge. He was a man of great investments, mainly in the Indies. He dealt in tobacco. I can only assume that he was murdered for the monies he would have had in his possession," Rose speculated.

"Would anyone have been forewarned of his arrival?" Gabriel asked.

"I'm sure if the family didn't know, then there are scarce others who would," she said in an irreverent tone.

Gabriel wasn't pleased with her answers and it showed. He would have to dig further and he wasn't a man to finely dress his investigations. He strode out of the room fully intending on putting some questions to the ones sitting just outside Caprington's walls.

Chapter 16

"*Can't you just get rid of him?" she asked blithely.*

"*I have thought of that, but you will have to give me more time to formulate a plan. Doing it now would raise too much suspicion. He has too many allies to get through to him and everyone is on high alert," he countered, hoping with all of his being that a battle ensued and his problem would be taken care of for him naturally.*

"*Well, then, if you think you've been careful enough, the only loose end lay upstairs in bed."*

"*We'll see. There are a few cards I can play," he said, seemingly more calm than he'd been since she'd known him. She took pause and wondered what he had planned and if it involved her.*

The girl was told no harm would come to her. William Colhoster took her from her mother's arms and thrust a note into her hand. She was to take the note to the men surrounding the castle that William had set his eyes on attaining.

"Go, girl. Daylight is wasting," he growled, shaking the hesitancy out of her. She couldn't resist one last look back at the huddled mass just inside the trees as she made her way across the glen. Her little legs carried her faster and faster toward her target, knowing that the sooner she did what she was told, the sooner she would be back with her mother.

Forging forward, mustering up her courage, she walked over the glen toward the men on horseback. It seemed like miles spanned between them as she walked. Reeds struck her bare legs making them itch. She batted at startled flying insects that flew around her with irritation. Fear grew in her throat making her thirsty as she gained ground closer to the men she was ordered to hand over the note.

Their armor was made of metal, not of wood and leather as her own clan. They towered over her as they sat aloft their horses with metal helmets shielding their faces from her with only small slats for them to see past. She imagined the man pulling off his helmet to reveal the face of a monster.

Shaking from fear and from cold, the girl stood staring up at the formidable soldier holding the flag of the king. His horse nickered, urging her to get on with her task, pulling her out of her daydream. As it began to rain, the drops fell on her face washing a bit of dirt into her eye. She immediately winced and rubbed at the irritation.

"Here, let me help you," the soldier next to the flag holder said. He dismounted and approached the girl, kneeling down before her. "Please don't be afraid. I won't cause you harm."

Volunteering a handkerchief, the soldier wiped her dirty face and eyes just as her mother or father would have. She no longer felt fear of him, just the flag holder who still shielded his monster face from her. She looked up at the man cleaning her face.

"I have a note for you," she said, holding out the piece of thin leather to the stranger.

"Thank you," he said and took the offered note. "How old are you?" he asked with a strained voice.

"Six. Can I go back to my mama?" she asked, already poised to run away from them.

"Yes," the soldier said after taking in the entirety of her dirty form. He watched as she ran off as fast as her little legs could carry her, back to the safety of her mother's arms. He took the note straight to his commander.

"She was only six, sir. How dastardly are these people to send a babe to contact the enemy? Have they no compunction?" he said, unable to hide his ire, being thoroughly affected by such callous behavior. He searched for reasoning behind the complete wrongness of such an act.

"On the contrary," Gabriel said as he read the crudely written note, "sending the child was their way of telling us they mean no malice and they trust we will discuss things peaceably. They want to meet."

"What are their terms?" Bernard asked.

"There were none stated. I have a feeling that this isn't a meeting of terms, dear fellow. This is a meeting to feel us out. They were taken aback by our presence and want to know our position. Get some horses. We're going to have a little chat with the neighbors." Gabriel threw the note on the table and strolled out of the room. He was looking forward to this.

Six unarmed men stood in the clearing awaiting reciprocity from the captain of the king's men who was inhabiting their mark. They ignored the rain that came in earnest, waiting, watching over puffs of frosted breath for the protectors of Caprington Castle to emerge.

Gabriel stopped the men a hundred yards away from the Colhoster council. Seeking to keep the peace, they dismounted and approached the other men who were dressed for this miserable weather. Thick fur-lined coats and hats protected them. It wouldn't protect them in battle.

"Have you come to announce your terms, my friend?" Gabriel spoke loudly to overcome the sound of the rain. A man of middle age came forward.

"I am William Colhoster. What interest is Caprington Castle to the king?" he spoke with a whisper of Scottish accent, a testament to his Scottish mother, no doubt.

"They are friends of mine and I will not let injustice be meted upon them. This attack is unwarranted." The men behind William began to talk among themselves, it was obvious to Gabriel that they came unprepared. His presence was a boon to Caprington's success against the Colhoster's eminent seizure.

"You well know sir that we have not attacked. We had just arrived to set about our campaign when you arrived."

"Watch yourself, Colhoster, for me and my men will haul you before King Henry himself if you speak falsehoods. Why have you come, if not to kill off the Boulstridges and claim their land for yourselves?" Gabriel accused, causing every one of the men to stop talking and look at the opposing group of men.

"I assure you, sir, to which you speak is untrue. We are not responsible for any death of the Boulstridges." William separated himself from the group and met Gabriel face to face. "As indecent as it is to admit, our sole purpose here was to press the women of the house to sell their land to us."

"Are you admitting to extortion?" Gabriel asked bluntly.

"No, I'm admitting to being very convincing. But if it means it will keep me from being accused of murder, then yes. Who may I ask was the unfortunate victim and by what means did they die?"

"Philip Boulstridge was found dead, murdered in the wood." Gabriel said, scrutinizing the man's face, examining his eyes.

"I'm saddened to hear of it. Please pass along my condolences to the family," he said with a furrowed brow.

"Do you also disclaim the poisonings of Kathryn Cunninghame and Elizabeth Hollingberry, then?" Gabriel asked. Shock covered the man's face. Gabriel knew he had nothing to do with either act before his denial.

"What are you about, sir? Are you accusing me of murdering a family for gain? At the most, all we've done is take advantage of a bad situation. We know that the Boulstridges are out of money and have good reason to sell their land. Our intent was to convince them to move elsewhere. We weren't going to take it out from under them without a cushion to fall on. We brought funds to compensate for their loss." William signaled for the money to be brought forth as proof. "And as further proof, search our camp. We've brought no weapons of war. The only weapons here are tools used to glean food from the forest."

Gabriel and William stood face to face for what seemed eternity. This man was telling the truth. Gabriel knew it in his bones. He sent out his men anyway, to obliterate any shred of doubt of their innocence. As presumed no weapons of war were found, no signs of poisons of any kind, no signs that these were people of malice. Women were cooking over open fires, children were playing, and dogs were running about. Not a scene you would find during hostile times.

"Take your people and go back from whence you came," Gabriel commanded, "or, by the power given to me by the king, I will remove you myself."

"If you will be so kind, sir, will you impart to me your name?" William asked, noting the decoration of the armor of which he wore.

"Gabriel Athelston of Laughtonwood."

William Colhoster immediately recognized the name and bowed his acquiescence. "I will, on your good name, be sure you will see to the justice of whoever has targeted the Boulstridge family. We will leave at sunrise."

"Before we part, I'd like to ask you about the destruction of your forge mill. I would like to survey the damage for myself," Gabriel declared authoritatively.

"There is nothing to see. It was completely demolished. Not a stone was left undamaged. I suspect we will be finding rubble for many miles," William retorted with a bitter tone.

"I would still like to survey the area for myself. I am looking for clues that may lead to the person committing these crimes," Gabriel said.

"You have free reign, sir. I will give you the only piece of evidence that you will ever find," William said, handing over a mutilated chunk of metal. "It was strange to me that we would find such a thing. It was in the middle of a crater that sat in what would have been the center of the mill. No one was there that day. McClatcher took his boys to visit their mother's grave site on this fifth anniversary."

With a firm grip on the second box associated with these explosions, Gabriel bid William good day and headed back to Caprington to collect his thoughts.

There was only one thing that kept his mind clear and his thoughts pure. That one thing, though, could also cost him his life if discovered by the wrong person. He closed himself off into his rooms after placing Bernard as guard, the only other person to know of his secret, carefully concealing it each time he sought its counsel. Satisfied with his chosen commission, he released his anxiety and allowed himself to be guided by another force.

True to his word, William Colhoster met Gabriel at the ruins of the forge mill. Within the rubble, the impressive crater was free of all debris surrounded by stone resembling nothing of a structure. The men stood back and surveyed the damage, one with the eye of loss and the other with the eye of scrutiny. Gabriel converged on the remains to dissect it for all it was worth.

"I don't suppose you will find the lid to the box, if that is what you are looking for," William said, skeptical of finding any usable evidence within the ruins.

"It would be nice, but that isn't my aim," Gabriel said, searching the surrounding area for the sign that someone ignited the explosion from nearby. It didn't take him long. The telltale black char mark ran from the rubble toward the forest. He followed the line and was pleasantly surprised by his find. "This is more than I'd hoped for, my friend. The person responsible not only left behind evidence, but I do believe he's injured."

Gabriel felt confident, armed with the blood stained rock before them, that his task just became infinitely easier. Unless the man was in hiding to heal his wounds, he would search him out with ease. Since there had been more vandalism after destroying this structure, it was obvious that it hadn't incapacitated him. More than likely the criminal was still among society.

Armed with this new information, Gabriel's vigor for searching the rubble thoroughly was reignited, netting him the find he could only have imagined. The lid to the box was laying inconspicuously within feet of the criminal's roost. He would add it to his growing collection of evidence.

Chapter 17

"LORD ATHELSTON, MAY I have a word with you?" Lilith called out from across the dining hall. Gabriel stopped to regard her with impatience, but thought better of brushing her off for the sake of keeping family ties cordial, for she had a determined set to her features and purposeful movements.

"Yes, Lady Hollingberry, you can. Actually, you may be of assistance to me," he said, holding his arm out for her to take while they travelled to a private place. "Please, discuss your purpose for searching me out."

"I know that it is not my place, but I feel that it is in Elizabeth's best interest to speak in her behalf. She is getting stronger and you may feel that it is within your entitlement to execute certain inalienable rights as her husband, but I am here to humbly request that you take heart and curb any needs for her sake," she said coyly, trying to convey her thoughts without too much embarrassment for either one of them.

"I beg your pardon, Lady Hollingberry?" Gabriel asked, trying to give Lilith the benefit of the doubt that she didn't mean to intimate that he was beyond controlling his male urges long enough to let her step-daughter recover before attacking her.

"It isn't that I doubt your chivalry, but I am aware of the baser needs of men," she admitted, holding her chin up in confidence that didn't meet her eyes. She was genuinely worried that he would push to consummate their marriage regardless of Elizabeth's condition.

"I assure you, Lady Hollingberry, I am and never will be such a barbarian to subject any woman to my 'baser needs' without being fully present in mind and body," he said reassuringly. Elizabeth is a beautiful woman and the prospect was not an unpleasant one, but one he wanted full participation with.

"Oh, thank you, Lord Athelston. I am sure this is a great sacrifice for a man of your stature," she said demurely with batting eyelashes and a comely smile.

Gabriel wasn't unschooled to women's wiles and saw through Lilith's ploy. He had the distinct feeling she had other, diversionary activities planned if her request had been refused. Dismissing his disgust, he diverted the conversation away from the current conversation to make headway with his investigation.

"Do you recognize this?" he asked, holding out the missing lid he'd found in the rubble. He was fortunate to find it nearly unscathed and intact with the exception of the scorched underside.

"It seems familiar, yes," she said, taking it from him and running her finger over the painted design. "Why don't we take it over to Edward. He will know of it.

"Yes, I recognize this very distinctly. It is a jewelry box I gave to Elizabeth several years ago. Why is it burned?" Edward asked.

"I'm sorry, Lord Hollingberry, but it was used in the destruction of the Colhoster's forge mill. This is the bottom portion," Gabriel said, producing the mutilated chunk of metal.

"That's odd. She didn't claim it to be missing," he said, unable to believe Elizabeth would be so careless as to be unaware of the keepsake.

"Since you recognize that one, maybe you will also recognize this one," Gabriel said, feeling hopeful.

"Well, it is the right size, but I can't be for certain since it is too damaged," Edward said, while examining the smaller box. Turning it over and examining it with a magnifying glass, making certain that it truly was whose he thought it was, he satisfied himself with every last detail confirmed. "This certainly does not bode well for Elizabeth."

Gabriel's mind ignited into instant suspicion of the woman he was now married. He questioned if he believed she was in criminal cabal with another, for he highly doubted she could have carried out these acts of vandalism unnoticed. Recalling her confession, he wasted no time gathering up the boxes and heading toward her room to question her.

Having witnessed the butler deliver a covered dish to her moments before, he took advantage of the timing to invite himself in. Gabriel was pleasantly surprised to see Elizabeth awake and sitting up. The maidservant was placing a bed tray before her, topped with a simple bowl of clear broth and a spoon.

"Lord Athelston," she said, surprised with his unannounced visit.

He stopped mid-stride and took in her appearance. She had lost considerable amount of weight for such a slight woman. Her cheeks were drawn and her eyes lacked luster. It seemed to take true effort to remain erect. Had she inflicted this upon herself for the sake of throwing the speculation elsewhere, or had her partner tried to get rid of her in effort to keep any spoils they were after?

"Good evening. Is this your first meal?" he asked, making sure his tone was cordial for the sake of an effective interview.

"Yes," she said, staring back at him with her hands resting in her lap.

"Then, if you would allow me the honor, I would like to stay as you dine." To his relief, she nodded her desire for him to stay. A chair materialized for him and he sat and watched her take her first sip of hot broth.

Elizabeth waited for her stomach to burn, to revolt, to do anything in adverse reaction to the new substance. The liquid slid across her tongue and down her throat to land warmly into her awaiting stomach with no ill effects. It was the best tasting broth she'd ever had. Not wanting to push her limits, she slowly consumed each bite.

Gabriel continued to watch after her. Noticing that she stopped only after consuming half of the broth, he urged her to continue and finish the entire bowl.

"I can't. I'm too tired. It took all the energy I had to eat what I have," she confessed, resolving to leave the rest.

"Then I'll help you," he found himself insisting. Feeding another person was foreign to Gabriel, but he tried his best. It wasn't as easy as he'd imagined it would have been. He ended up spilling a portion of the first spoonful or two on Elizabeth before he got the hang of it. It was surprising to Gabriel how intimate he felt feeding her. She must have felt it too, for it was difficult for her to keep his gaze. Each time she opened her mouth, though, she looked into his eyes and opening her mouth for him, allowing him to give her nourishment. It was a heady feeling and he relished every moment and thought of the conversation he and Lilith had just moments prior.

"Thank you," she said after blotting the corners of her mouth, barely able to keep her eyes open.

"You're very welcome." He handed the empty tray to the maid and returned to his seat. "Before you return to rest, Miss Elizabeth, I have some questions for you."

Gabriel produced both boxes. Studying her reaction, he was surprised when she reached out and took them from him without hesitation. She readily identified the jewelry box, but paid more than the usual attention to the smaller box, staring at it as if seeing a ghost. She couldn't mask what Gabriel interpreted as hurt, emotional pain along with shock at the destruction of the item.

"Where did you find these?" she asked.

"The small one was used to ignite the barracks at Sir Hessencastle's estate," he said matter-of-factly. Shock and disbelief crossed her face as she held it tight to her chest.

"What about the jewelry box?"

"It was used in destroying the Colhoster's forge mill."

"I can't believe it. Who would do such a thing?" she asked with righteous indignation.

"I would suppose you should tell me. By all rights, this looks like you have something to do with both incidents." Gabriel stood, using his height to try to intimidate her.

"But I didn't. I would never destroy something so precious to me, let alone destroy someone else's property! This trinket box was given to me by my mother, who received it from her mother. It was beautiful. It had a stained glass lid with a dragonfly on it. I would never destroy such a precious memento," she said tearfully at his audacious statement.

"Then explain it to me. I know that they are yours, that you have free reign to travel all over the countryside unchecked and that you are familiar with all of the families involved. The only thing I have yet to discover is a motive," he stated as if he'd convinced himself of her guilt regardless of her denial. His countenance turned as dark as his coloring in a blink of an eye, making Elizabeth nervous.

"You cannot believe that I would do such a thing! I had nothing to do with any of it. Yes, I have been to each of these estates, but nowhere near the places that were vandalized, I'm familiar with the families because we are a close-knit community and have known each other since I was born. I have no motive because there is none to be had. I have nothing against my neighbors, nor do they have anything against us," she said as she pushed the covers away and stood on her knees to face him in her ire, not realizing that she was just in her night dress.

Despite his better judgment, Gabriel allowed his eyes to linger over Elizabeth's form as she ranted. He supposed his mind was primed to think of his baser needs, but he couldn't keep himself from wondering if she truly was too weak and fragile take this instant. He cursed his promise to abstain from marital relations until she was fully recovered.

"What about your confession?" he asked, taking a step closer to the bed.

"What confession?"

"The other day when you woke, you said that it was your fault. Why did you say that if you weren't involved with this?" he asked, gesturing toward the boxes.

"I assure you, Lord Athelston, that I do not know what you speak of," she said defiantly.

"Who are you trying to protect?" he demanded with an imposing presence, standing over her in an intimidating fashion.

"No one," she countered, wanting to plead her innocence but feeling her desire to quarrel with him wane the closer he came and she became instantly aware of her predicament. "I swear, I'm not the one you are looking for."

He stood above her as she knelt on her bed staring up at him with her large, anxious eyes and trembling body. Yes, he told himself, she was the one he'd been looking for as he wrapped his arm around her waist lowered his lips to hers, but she wasn't so inclined.

"Quit backing away, Elizabeth. I'm not going to bite you," he said, noting her increased breathing and uncertainty. Smiling at her reluctance, seeing it as a good sign, he placed his other hand behind her head and guided her to him. She was sweet and hot, searing him with her skin. Her lips were soft and young. He felt as if her hand she'd placed over his heart was burning through his tunic in effort to brand it.

Tearing himself away from her, he stepped back for fear of breaking his promise in short order. He wasn't sure she could handle the rigors of love making the way he wanted it at this moment and wanted to spare both of them the frustration of an unfulfilling experience.

Turning on his heel, Gabriel sped out of the room in search of answers. He was going to get to the bottom of this matter as quickly as possible. If she was involved with this he would find out-and then she would feel the brunt of his anger, but until then, he was going to keep searching.

Elizabeth was left in wonder about this man that was now her husband, trying to understand his quick change in demeanor and rapid change from caring thoughtfulness to accusing condescension to tender and loving. Her thoughts automatically leapt to Sir Lincoln and wondering if he would survive his son's behavior being of fragile mind. A protective instinct came over her as she fell asleep. She would do anything she could to protect such a gentle, mild man such as he. She wouldn't bear to see him hurt any more than he already was.

Chapter 18

"GABRIEL, YOU CAN'T possibly be insinuating that Elizabeth is entangled with the inherent evil that has been occurring in Suffolk as of late! That's preposterous!" Caleb argued.

"Then explain to me how it is an impossibility when I have evidence in my hand that she is at least knowing of the one committing these crimes," Gabriel demanded.

"I can't, not about the boxes, but I do know that she is not the kind of woman that could do as you claim. I have known her for years and she is a lifelong friend of my wife's whose judgment in character is infallible. I declare that you will not find anything lacking in Elizabeth's conduct that would warrant such an accusation," Caleb said, surprised that he had to defend his wife's good friend against such slander.

"Women can be both beguiling and yet deceiving Caleb. I cannot dismiss any inclination of guilt just because she is female or conducts herself well before others. I will dig until her innocence is proven," Gabriel said, dismissing the disheartened look in his friend's eyes.

"Gabriel, my friend, you can't do this to yourself," Caleb said, noticing the automatic stiffness in Gabriel's stance. He was bracing himself to hear the words and Caleb obliged. "She isn't your mother."

Stifling instinct to argue that all women were like his mother, Gabriel decided to do the next best thing. He left the room without a word in effort to preserve their friendship. His thoughts turned black as memories flooded his mind of their own accord.

"I have not yet found the source of the poisoning yet. I fear that we never will. Everything has been tested and, without a doubt, there has been no reaction from the animals except in getting plump." Bernard said, giving full disclosure.

"Lady Hollingberry and Wesley have assured me that Elizabeth's strength is returning, although I haven't seen any such signs. Maybe it's time to remove ourselves and return the Hollingberry's to their home where she can convalesce and I can continue my investigation."

"Pecor," he shouted needlessly, for the man was never far from his commander's side.

"Yes sir." He rounded the corner into the study and stood ready for his next edict.

"Choose from the men five hundred to stay behind here. The rest are to accompany me to Listhenshire. We leave tomorrow at dawn."

"Am I to be one of the five hundred, sir?"

"No, Wiggins will be left in charge. Make him aware that these people are to have the training to defend themselves by the time we leave for Piffenview. Make weapons and teach them how to use them. I want them to be ready just in case the unthinkable happens."

A buzz started throughout Caprington as the troops readied themselves to move out the next morning. It was Edward who came to Elizabeth's room where Lilith and Wesley were dutifully watching over her that informed them of the decision to return home was made. Elizabeth could have sworn there was a distinct worried look that passed between mother and son.

"May I ride beside you?" Wesley asked as he kept his horse even with Gabriel's, who gave no reply. "I hear you have a younger brother my age, is that right?"

"That's right." Gabriel continued watching the horizon, not wanting to deal with Wesley at the moment. He'd had enough of the boy lurking around corners and doorways and was sure he was up to no good. There was something about him that didn't sit right.

In the past, Gabriel's sense of people's character was uncanny, an asset the king used to his advantage, yet when it was directed toward Wesley he talked himself out of listening to that tiny voice inside him. The boy seemed too young to be labeled as a miscreant, or even reprobate. He was young and unschooled in the ways of manhood.

Wesley, in Gabriel's estimation, was a dandy, a fop, and a gadder. He seemed to have no purpose in life except for doing what he was told. Left to his own devices, a boy like Wesley could wind up in the bowels of the king's prison. In time he may grow out of it, but he seriously doubted it would be anytime soon. The boy needed stern direction and made to think for himself. Without self-reliance, a poor soul could get lost and never find the proper way to go. Gabriel turned his attention to Wesley and decided then and there to impart whatever influence he could on the growing boy. It was his duty as brother-in-law to help this unfortunate pup.

"Maybe I can introduce you when they return from London." Wesley smiled in response.

Riding in the carriage with Elizabeth, Lilith was able to see Wesley followed her instruction to befriend Gabriel. A certain triumphant feeling came over her knowing that her plan was coming along nicely. She sat back to enjoy the remainder of the trip home in peace and quiet, mentally formulating plan after contingency plan. Failure was not an option.

The house was prepared to receive its owners as well as its temporary guests. Gabriel and his men were greeted rather informally which, under the circumstances, was understandable. Elizabeth was gathered and swept up into her rooms. Edward, who offered a wholehearted welcome and an extended stay to his son-in-law and all his men, oriented him to the inner workings of the household.

He was escorted to his rooms which were as far away from Elizabeth's as humanly possible. He was not pleased to say the least, but rather than rail about miniscule affairs Gabriel contented himself in searching the household before questioning the servants.

There was no evidence anywhere that would indicate the manufacturing or storage of any amount of arsenic in the Hollingberry household. Searching every room possible, Gabriel was satisfied that no physical space had been unsearched.

"We found nothing, sir. The only chemicals found were paints in an outbuilding," Wiggins informed him.

"There is little arsenic used in paints, if at all. I highly doubt that would be the source," Gabe replied, hoping to find more than a pinch of the substance.

"The paints were hand-made with no indication he used arsenic, sir, but the paintings are spectacular."

"I'll be sure to view them later. First, I have an appointment to speak with the cook," he said, hoping for the smallest of leads.

The cook stood before Gabriel with a pleasant look of worry on her face. A short, round woman of later years stood proud as she approached this new guest and protector. "Is there anything I can make special for you, kind sir, a sweet perhaps or a special request of your liking?"

"No, Mrs. White. I came to talk to you about the condition of Elizabeth Hollingberry." An instant frown covered her face, reaching her eyes. "Somehow, Mrs. White, the ladies had been poisoned."

"Yes, I am aware of that. It is quite a shame. It couldn't have happened to a sweeter, more docile creature." Sorrow ran through her voice, her face, and her mannerisms.

"Yes." Gabriel remained quiet, allowing her time to make the mental leap of his request to speak with her. Obviously she wasn't so inclined, for she stood there with fretting hands, her frown deepening as she contemplated the fact of his statement. "Mrs. White, I need to know from whom you purchased your goods from. Do you know these vendors well?"

"I always buy from the same vendors, and yes, I trust them," she said, continuing to unconsciously rub her hands together as she recited a list of vendors from memory. "I've used them long before I came to work for the Hollingberrys. They wouldn't risk selling inferior product, let alone poisoned. They would be run out. No one would purchase their goods!"

"Indeed. What about your staff, Mrs. White. Have you any new staff members as of late?'

"No. Not unless you define recent as fifteen years ago. Are you suggesting that someone here may have poisoned the Boulstridges?" she asked, incredulously.

Gabriel ignored her and continued with questioning. "Mrs. White, do you oversee all the makings of the household and their guests receive?"

"Yes, sir, there isn't a single thing entering this dining room that isn't first approved by me. From start to presentation, I make most everything they consume. At larger parties there are more people involved for all practical purposes, but with daily family meals, I am the sole food preparer," she said with a flare of indignation in her voice.

"So, if there were foul play, you would be a person of interest." It was a statement meant to judge her reaction, which garnered a resounding gasp and a look of ghastly mortification at the thought that she would do such a thing.

"Sir, I assure you that nothing of that nature would *ever* be of consequence in my household. If you think I could do that to a family such as the Hollingberry family, a family I've been employed with for more than thirty years, or to the Boulstridges for that matter, you are sadly mistaken." She dearly wished she could have slapped the face that just insulted her and stomp off in righteous indignation, but she knew full well that would mean her job, or worse yet, the king would have her head.

Gabriel stood silent, giving her a narrow-eyed glare, judging her every word. After five heartbeats, he resigned his inquisition. "Very well, I believe you." The cook loosed a captured breath. "You do understand that everything, and everyone, must come under speculation and it's my duty to see to it that justice be served."

"I understand. Although I'm not fond of being the target of such speculation, I'm aware that all angles must be investigated." She harrumphed and added, "I highly doubt you have to look too far past the north boundary to find your culprits, though," she said as she waddled off to inform the kitchen staff of their entire conversation.

"I must say, browbeating the servants is your forte," Bernard said as he entered the room.

"Did you find anything of consequence?" Gabriel asked, not wanting to discuss the matter.

"Yes, but I don't know how it relates to the issue at hand. Elizabeth has three lady's maids who are well trained and say next to nothing. The butler looks at me as if I'm a traitor for asking him the simplest of questions, and even Elizabeth seems to be quieter. There is a feel to this house that isn't right," Bernard offered.

"Send the butler in to me."

"Yes, sir, I do believe I am involved with the unfortunate poisoning of my mistress," Darwin answered with a resounding voice laced with deep sorrow. "I put it in with her things, but I do not know who made them. The tin was sitting on the side table here," he indicated with a slow, sweeping gesture before bringing his hand up to catch a tear.

"Who would have put it there?"

"I honestly cannot think of a single person, sir," he said, recalling the sight of Elizabeth in her weakened state.

"Has anything unusual or untoward happened within the family that you can tell me? Do they get along?" Gabriel asked in hopes of finding a motive.

"Everything was placid and serene until Wesley came home from university. Before that nothing untoward has happened for many years. Lord Hollingberry tended to business while Lady Hollingberry spent most of her time in the gardens or the hot houses. Miss Elizabeth managed the household and painted. Everything was as it should be," he said forlornly, longing for those days of grace when nothing was wrong with his household.

"What happened upon Wesley's arrival?"

"He has proven upsetting to the household sir, demonstrating himself to be quite the menace. He's played tricks on the family, fallen off horses and even mishandled a sword and stabbed Lord Hollingberry. He puts me ill at ease, sir."

"Yes, I remember. I'll be sure to include him in training sessions with the men to toughen him and increase his skill," he said, hoping that such a measure would also help him to mature. "Is there any link, no matter how small, you can make with Elizabeth and the crimes being committed around Suffolk?" Gabriel asked, knowing just what a reception he would receive. With the worshipful way the butler said her name, Gabriel knew that the man would not implicate Elizabeth even if he knew of direct fact.

"No, sir, I do not," he said with stone features.

"I thought as much. Your loyalty is noted."

"It is not merely loyalty, Lord Athelston, it is fact. Please, examine me and I will tell you of her whereabouts upon each instance. I cannot let the name of my mistress to go smeared, even if by her husband. She is as innocent as a child as you will see if you spend any amount of time with her," Darwin stated with more force than Gabriel imagined he had in him.

"I can see that you will champion her regardless of my speculations. Can I even expect you to answer my questions honestly? You can barely take a full step, how can I expect you to know where she goes and with whom she meets?" Gabriel scoffed.

"You forget, sir, what a small community this is. I also beg you to recall that I was around when your grandfather was alive. I know all that is going on with my mistress," he defended without remorse.

"Duly noted. Tell me what I should know about Lady Elizabeth and these boxes," Gabriel asked, bringing the items to the old man's attention. It took him a moment to recognize the objects, but he was sure of their history.

"The jewelry box was being fixed. She took it to the smithy just a fortnight ago after noticing a crack in the pearl inlay. She wanted him to line the lid with a metal plate in order to support the pearl. It had been a gift from her father and was precious to her, but not as precious as this one." The old butler gingerly ran his fingers over the gnarled metal with a bitter-sweet smile on his face.

"She told me it was a memento from her mother. Did she use it for anything?" Gabriel asked, pulling the butler out of his reverie.

"No she didn't. She was only eleven when her dear mother died and it broke her heart. She said she wanted to leave it empty to remind her of the emptiness it resembled in her heart. It was only two years ago that she placed it in her dowry chest, safely tucked away with her mother's wedding dress."

Gabriel continued questioning Darwin until he was satisfied. It was completely plausible that Elizabeth was being framed for such activities, but why? Neither of them could create an answer. He spoke with every single servant he could find and questioned them as well with no progress. It was time for him to contemplate his next move.

Chapter 19

"I'M SENDING HALF the troops ahead of us. Lord Garrott will be wondering what is causing our delay. At least this will give him some good faith that I and the remainder of my men will be replacing him and his faction shortly," Gabriel told Bernard and Justin during the noon meal.

"Wiggins tells me that Caprington is almost ready to stand on its own two feet," Justin reported.

"Good because I want you and Wiggins to be part of the two thousand," he stated positively. Justin gave a curt nod in acceptance. "Maybe things will be less stressful to the family without so many of us about," Gabriel mused.

"Do you think our presence is really stressing them too much?" Bernard asked. "Most of us are camped far away from the castle and few within the walls."

"Mrs. Hollingberry has voiced her angst a time or two that she feels our presence is pressing in on her and the family. Both Lord and Lady Hollingberry have suggested that we take our leave and when Elizabeth recovers she will be sent along after us," Gabriel informed.

"Are you inclined to do so?" Justin asked.

"Decidedly not! I give Elizabeth consideration seeing what she has gone through, but she is gaining strength daily. I will not leave without her." Gabriel dismissed Justin with his instructions and became involved in his own thoughts.

"Is something on your mind?" Bernard asked, seeing the furrowed brow and lost gaze as an indication of Gabriel's downward thoughts.

"I need more time to investigate this than originally planned. Tomorrow I will head out to talk with the townsfolk and the authorities. Tonight, though, I plan on dining with my wife," Gabriel admitted.

"Be careful, my friend, you might find yourself liking her," Bernard said with a smile.

"Doubtful," he replied.

They were served Saxe-Coburg soup, much to the delight of Gabriel, who was glad to see Elizabeth take a bit of meat, even if it were finely cut bits of ham. He wondered how long she would have to remain on a diet of soup before she fully regained her strength. A healing body needs more than just soup and cider.

Gabriel refrained from speaking until she had emptied her bowl. She lingered over the task at hand tonight, seemingly hesitant in initiating any conversation during the meal. After inquiring of the quality of her meal, Gabriel ventured into engaging her in a different way.

"I want to do something tonight. You may think it rather unconventional, but I hope you'll humor me."

"All right," she reluctantly consented. Tonight she was fully dressed, no longer wanting to present her husband with her entire collection of dressing gowns.

"If you may, I'd like to take this journey out onto the terrace." Gabriel stood and took hold of his chair, effortlessly carrying it to a spot he thought perfect for her and saw her comfortably seated before he began. "I want you to look up at the moon and see how round and full it is." She did as he directed. "Now, take in a deep breath and close your eyes."

To his amazement, seeing her face fully illuminated by the moon was something he wasn't prepared to see. Its light cast an ethereal glow to her skin and it saturated her every pore. The stark contrast of her dark, chestnut brown hair made her look like a Greek goddess he'd seen in paintings and captured within sculptures. If he believed such things, he would have easily labeled her Nyx, the goddess of night. He had to physically pull himself away from her and look out in the darkness to clear his head.

It felt good to Elizabeth to fill her lungs with the cool night air. Its cleansing properties helped stay her nerves as Gabriel stood over her, staring at her. Even though she had her eyes closed, she could feel his eyes on her. It made her heart race contemplating his nearness and his interest in her. Secretly she wished he would steal a kiss as she sat and waited to expose his purpose of pulling her out into the night.

"I want to give you a mental picture," he began slowly, drawing out each and every syllable. "You're at a magnificent castle made just for you. Picture yourself on a parapet, far above the ground. You can see for miles and miles, but instead of rolling green hills dotted with sheep and cattle, before you is the wondrous North Sea. You hear the seagulls call to you as they search for their next meal. You smell and taste the salty sea air." Gabriel was pleased as she inhaled deeply once more. She'd allowed herself to travel with him.

"Turn around and you see the castle yard with a stone wall that spans for miles and miles. There's no end to it. It holds within its walls all its people, safe and sound. The castle itself is sprawled out over at least fifty acres. You can see five towers, the courtyard, as well as a garden that takes your breath away." With caution, Gabriel chanced a glimpse. Elizabeth was smiling, reveling in the freedom to 'see' such magnificent grounds of the 'castle made just for her'. "Going inside, the first thing you notice is the well-appointed paintings, your paintings. They grace the walls wherever you go. Whatever you choose to see, that is what it is. Every table in every room boasts fresh bouquets of flowers."

"Your rooms are well appointed with gold and emerald green. You have dresser upon wardrobe full of gowns of every kind. Off to one side is a private bathing room, complete with a marble tub and a hearth big enough to stand in. Your anteroom will always be full of friends awaiting you to have tea and scones. And, of course, you have your studio close by. It will only suffice to have the best lighting and enough room for you to create whatever is your heart's desire."

Gabriel continued on and on through the dining hall, ballrooms, the library and the many features he so clearly described to her. She was so ensconced in the mental journey that she envisioned every detail vividly and with amazing clarity as if she were present amidst this magical place.

"The best thing, though, is that this place really does exist. That is where we will live, Piffenview." Gabriel lifted her delicate hand and kissed it.

At first, Gabriel was unsure if Elizabeth was going to react to him. He supposed it took a moment for her to grasp the idea of living in such a magnificent place, but then her smile reached into her eyes and shone brightly. She couldn't remain seated or withhold her arms from reaching around his neck for an embrace.

"Why are you crying?" he asked forlornly.

"Because I'm so happy and so proud of you," she said with genuine happiness.

"You are proud of me? You don't even know me," he said, not understanding this queer feeling that overcame him. It was rather unique and novel.

"To be appointed to such a position must be a great honor. It speaks well of you. You must have worked hard to be granted such an impressive assignment. It shows the trust the king has in you and your abilities," she explained. She wondered if she offended him, having received a furrowed brow for her compliment, then relaxed as a smile covered his face.

Gabriel was in uncharted territory. He realized that in this solitary moment with Elizabeth, he received his first order of verbal praise he could remember. He couldn't recall ever being told that someone was proud of him, not even his parents. He had expectations to meet since the day he was born, a position which didn't lend itself to much praise.

Even though Gabriel hated to, he separated himself from Elizabeth and left her to rest. He instantly felt as though his very warmth was stolen from him. He consoled himself with a pint of ale and then suffered through dinner before coming to the conclusion that he needed to see her once more before he retired for the night. Even if she were asleep he wanted to gaze upon her sweet face so he could dream about her softly folded within his arms.

Gabriel knocked softly. When no one answered, he knocked harder, still no answer. Knowing of the three maids in constant attendance, he became concerned. He tried the knob, only to find it locked. Instantly infuriated, Gabriel yelled for the key to Elizabeth's room be brought forth.

"Where is she?" he bellowed, only to have the maid so in fear of him that she was unable to answer him. When the key was produced and the door opened, he searched her room, unable to locate her. His temper flared uncontrollably. "Find her!"

"Miss Elizabeth, come quickly. Lord Athelston is looking for you and he seems mighty angry." The maid ushered her along the servant's entrances, not allowing her to stop to rest as before, but pulling her along by the hand. Elizabeth tried to keep up with Winnie, to hurry back before Gabriel became too angry, tripping twice on the hem of her gown.

The servant's stairwell was too narrow to pass through at a good pace. They had to go through the kitchen and up the main stairs in order to make better time. How was she going to explain matters to Gabriel? It would draw suspicion for sure, and if she chose to tell Gabriel of the crime against her, Elizabeth could only fathom what would happen. She would leave with him soon, taking Charlotte with her, which would eliminate any retribution if her speculations were correct. She would have to keep her secret for the sake of life.

Reaching the top of the stairs, Winnie stopped and peeked around the corner to see if Gabriel stood sentry. Noting the hallway was empty, the two proceeded to sneak toward her door, careful not to draw attention. Elizabeth reached her room without hindrance and quickly entered, shutting and locking the door, leaving Winnie and the others having to knock if they wished to enter.

"Where have you been?" Gabriel asked startling Elizabeth. He had been on the terrace waiting for her. Knowing she had to return to her room, he opted to stay instead of traipsing throughout the castle looking for the chit. How easily his original thinking returned to the feeling that there was something more to Elizabeth than appeared to the eye. Old habits reared their ugly heads and surfaced just in time for her to look as guilty as sin.

"Please, don't ask me," she pleaded. "Don't ask what I cannot answer." Her back was to the wall, literally and figuratively.

"You gave me the impression that you were too weak to leave your rooms. Is that so, Elizabeth?" he asked pointedly.

"I have been gaining strength, but I choose to expend it sparingly," she admitted. The jaunt up the stairs and the stress of the situation had leached her strength and she felt it wane. She crossed to the chair beside the hearth and sat.

"And what, or whom, did you choose to expend it on tonight?" He glared at her as he closed the distance between them.

"Please, I cannot confess," she appealed earnestly.

"Confess to what?" He stood before her with barely controlled fury. He leaned forward, placing his hands on either side of the arms of the chair, leaning into her. "That you've been having an affair?" Gabriel was taken aback by the speed and ferocity of Elizabeth's slap, but he was glad of it.

"Don't you *ever* say that to me again!" she fumed, meaning every word, tears threatening to spill from her eyes. Her eyes were molten lava as she pushed the words out from between her lips. Gabriel stood and rubbed the offended cheek.

"I beg your pardon. When I find my wife not in her rooms at night and sneaking around, my mind couldn't separate this world from the world I was in at court." He could see by the set of her jaw that she wasn't about to accept the reasoning behind his harsh accusation. "I should go." He retired his attempt to find the real reason she was absent from her rooms until another time. He unlocked the door and exited without a backward glance.

As he lay in his bed that night, he reviewed the night's encounter with Elizabeth, replaying every scene, reviewing every word, recalling every facial expression. She was so passionate about refuting his accusation of infidelity that, now that he thought about it, could have been interpreted to the positive or the negative.

Gabriel tossed and turned, agitated with this riddle. Right before sleep claimed his thoughts, though, he wondered what it meant to him that Elizabeth locked her door even before he was two steps away from her doorway.

Chapter 20

"Ay I speak with you, sir?" Wesley spoke from the doorway of Edward's study. Edward had been busy with paperwork all morning and needed a break from penning his business partners, alerting them to the disaster befalling their neighbors and his subsequent delay in handling business matters until Elizabeth's recovery. Edward returned the quill to its holder thinking that he would rather have any other interruption than Wesley at this moment.

"Let me get a drink first," Edward sighed, needing the liquid fortification it afforded. Wesley was compliant as he patiently waited for his step-father to pour himself a drink, gulp it down, then refilled his glass before returning to the opposite side of his desk. Wesley wasn't offered any brandy, nor did he ask for any.

"I must make a confession," he started, having to build up the nerve. He stammered and paced with his hands behind his back. He stopped several times only to return to his pacing. Finally, Edward was growing tired of Wesley's antics and bellowed for him to get on with it.

"This isn't a light subject, I fear. I'm having a difficult time finding just the right words."

"Well, you should have thought about that before disturbing me. If you don't spit it out, go away and then come back when you have the right words. This infernal pacing is giving me a headache."

"Elizabeth and I are having an affair!" he said, blurting out what he'd come to say.

At first, Edward gave a chuckle, thinking Wesley was making a joke. When he saw the boy's face with all seriousness, even perspiring for the effort of it, he thought more seriously of the boy's statement.

"I doubt it, boy. I don't doubt that you'd be inclined to do so, but I think higher of Elizabeth. She wouldn't sully herself with the likes of you."

"It's true, sir. Several weeks ago, while she went out to the marsh to paint, we met and displayed our feelings for each other," he said, looking like he was about to throw up.

Edward thought about what Wesley was saying. He had to take a deep breath in effort for his chest not to crush his heart as he contemplated a quandary such as this and the scandal it would bring upon the family. What if the king decided to take retribution on Lord Athelston's behalf and reserve Elizabeth for the guillotine? Edward moved toward the sideboard once more for more fortification.

Edward couldn't believe such a situation existed between his beloved daughter and a whelp like Wesley. He resolved to discuss this privately with her after this next drink when a thought occurred to him. As the tumbler stopped half-way to its mark, a smile crept onto his face. This was just what he needed. He would defend Elizabeth from the king's wrath, all the while Elizabeth could stay here with him, by his side as she'd promised.

Yes, that was it, she was fulfilling her promise to stay with him for the rest of her life, but found herself saddled with a husband. Yes, this was the only way she could keep her promise. Edward's eyes became misty with feelings of love for his baby daughter.

"I thought it best to speak with you now, before anything was said to Gabriel about this. Do you think it wise to tell Gabriel soon?" Wesley asked as he trembled in fear.

"Why do you ask? Is there some rush that he know of your sin?" Edward didn't mince words, for he wanted to be rid of the idea of his beloved baby daughter and this sniveling boy even if it netted him what he wanted. He still couldn't imagine the two being romantically inclined, let alone lovers.

"No, no rush." Wesley finally planted himself in the leather chair facing Edward's desk, seemingly searching for his next words. "It's just that having him around makes me nervous. I want to know when you are going to tell him so I can be prepared."

"To hide, you mean." It was a statement of character, not a question.

"No," Wesley said quickly, but it was his intention to not be anywhere near Gabriel, a highly lethal military man, after he heard the tale that would seal their fates. "I mean I want to be prepared. What if he decides to call me out for a duel?"

That notion was quite pleasant to Edward. He knew who would be the victor, and justly so. Wesley, no doubt pursued Elizabeth with intent. Even though Elizabeth had a good head on her shoulders, she was still just a female and unused to the advances of men. Still, he thought of her as above such things. He stared into his brandy and contemplated his next move.

"I'm not going to tell him," he announced, lowering the boom on Wesley, "you are."

Panic struck Wesley to the quick. His thoughts swam in a dizzying whirlpool in his brain, unable to form a response. How was he going to pull something like that off without getting himself killed?

"Is there a problem, Wesley?" Edward asked, noting the color draining from his step-son's face. When Wesley didn't answer, but continued to stare at the floor, he knew the boy wasn't going to confess anytime soon. "It's the ultimate test of manhood, boy." Edward realized he liked goading him. Feeling the weight of the world lifted off his shoulders, Edward finished his brandy with a flare and let the glass land with a thud on the desk, making Wesley jump.

"No, there's no problem. It just changes things." Wesley stood and slowly walked to the door. "I have some things to think about," he said, excusing himself and trotting toward the door.

Edward had to smile from self-satisfaction. He could see it now: Wesley would confess to Gabriel, a seasoned soldier who would likely take physical retribution from the boy, obtain a certificate of divorce posthaste, leaving Elizabeth here to live out her days beside her aging yet benevolent father. It was the best scenario he could have hoped for in this situation. The family would endure the scandal and, in time, Elizabeth's reputation would be set to rights. Yes, he was positive it would all work itself out.

"You *didn't*!" Bernard's worst fears came true as his friend confessed his sins, as well as his angst regarding the night before.

"I'm sure I did, for I had a mighty sting on my left cheek afterward."

"It serves you right!" Bernard barked at his friend. Gone were their roles as commander to officer. They had doffed their positions long ago in lieu of donning a stronger than brotherhood friendship. "Just because she was not where you expected her to be doesn't mean she was having a torrid fling. I swear, Gabriel, the king's court has colored your vision too thoroughly."

"But she wouldn't account for her absence. She said she couldn't 'confess'. What am I supposed to do with that except to assume she is involved in wrongdoing?" he asked, willing the vice around his heart to loosen.

"Is that all being at court taught you?" Bernard stood and placed closed fists on the desk, checking his burgeoning outrage at the thick-headedness of his friend. "Have you been so blinded by all those disloyal to you, whose goal was to do something bad that you disregarded the thousands around you that were genuine?"

"I don't know where you were while I was within the Palace of Placentia protecting the king, Cabrera. If you'd have been there, you would have noted that *everyone* had an agenda. Everyone had something to attain. Everyone had their ways and means to get what they wanted." Even though Gabriel's tone was even and trained, there was an unmistakable hardness that loomed in his eyes. He believed with every fiber of his being that there could be nothing but an ominous ending to this riddle.

Bernard was set to prove him wrong. He had to pay Elizabeth a visit first.

"Mr. Cabrera." Elizabeth smiled and indicated for him to take the vacant seat opposite her beside the fire.

"Please, call me Bernard."

"And you may call me Elizabeth. Have you come to examine me again?"

"No, this is more of a social visit. I thought you would appreciate seeing a new face from time to time." He was rewarded with a pleasant smile. "Tell me, how have you been feeling lately?"

"My strength has been improving daily."

"Good." Trying to arrange the needed conversation in his head, Bernard let the silence between them settle to find a comfortable spot. He imagined asking her a myriad of questions, following her if she left her rooms, or even telling her his plight in proving Gabriel wrong in order to get down to the truth.

"Bernard," she spoke softly, timidly, "I need to ask you a queer question."

"You may ask me anything, Elizabeth."

"Have you spoken with my Lord Athelston today?"

"Yes."

"Did he mention anything about an altercation yesterday?" She tried to hide the milling of her fingers within her skirt, but Bernard noticed.

"He mentioned something, yes."

"What did he say?" She swallowed hard as she waited for his reply.

"He was worried about you, Elizabeth. When you weren't in your room late at night, his thoughts ran in the only course he's known for the past ten years." Bernard perched himself on the edge of his seat, leaning forward as if he were imparting a very special piece of information to her. "You see Gabriel is part of an elite team meant to ferret out people who are against the king and his throne. That can entail anything from political maneuvering, to defrauding of any kind, to manipulation of the royal family in any way. He was in charge of investigating and ousting those who attempt to disrupt the king's rule."

"Oh." She absorbed the information as best she could within her own situation. She had to be extra careful around him.

"Was that the answer you were looking for?"

"Actually, no." She pulled her thoughts back to the man sitting across from her. "I was wondering if he mentioned any injury I may have caused him."

Bernard's brows drew together. "No, he didn't mention any-" Bernard withdrew his words and quickly thought of the conversation. "Do you mean the slap?" Elizabeth recoiled as if just mentioning the incident caused her pain.

"Yes. I didn't mean to hurt him, it just happened in the heat of the moment. I wasn't thinking properly when I struck him. It was inappropriate of me.

"My dear," Bernard smiled, first at the tenderness she was showing and second at the thought of her being able to injure a man like Gabriel, "I don't think he's any worse for wear. Regardless of his deservedness of the strike, Gabriel is a seasoned soldier. I think he could withstand any assault he merits by your hand without injury," he reassured her. "Emotionally, though, he needs a little more training."

"Training you say?"

"Gabriel needs to learn to trust. Since he's been surrounded by people who always pretend to be something else, he views almost everyone as dishonest and untrustworthy, always having ulterior motives. He also has personal experience with unfaithfulness that makes him especially untrusting."

"Yes, I am aware that his mother ran off with another man when he was but a boy." She could only imagine what Gabriel felt as a little boy in that instance. As she thought about him and what Bernard just told her, she came to wonder. "Has he ever come across someone who was innocent?"

"I can't say that for sure. He had to be secretive about his investigations, you understand. He couldn't tell me about the details especially if they were matters dealing with the security of the throne."

"I see." She withdrew from the conversation and returned to gaze at the flames.

With the silent dismissal, Bernard looked back at the conversation and wondered what it was about her that Gabriel found so distrusting. If he only would open his eyes, he would see that, yes, there was something more to her, but not in the sense Gabriel concluded. He would have to try to convince Gabriel of that very thing. He left without a clue how to accomplish that very feat.

"Girls," Elizabeth informed her maids collectively, "I've made a decision. Tonight I won't be dining in my room. Inform the staff that I'll be dining alone in the morning room. I also wish to have something more substantial than soup," she said, feeling invigorated at the thought of getting out of her rooms, even if it were for a short time.

"But, my lady, what about Sir Athelston?" the maid asked.

"I highly doubt he will be interested in dining with me tonight after last night's escapade." The repellant situation in which she'd found herself propelled her forward into more daring ambitions. "I'm going to see Charlotte now."

The decision felt like defiance. For the past week, sneaking down the servant's passageways late in the night was for a purpose. She needed to see to the emotional support of Charlotte, the one who sustained injuries as a result of protecting her mistress, and for her own sanity. Even though Charlotte wasn't speaking to her, Elizabeth was sure she gained strength just by being present at her bedside keeping vigil even in her own delicate state.

In her mind's eye if she were in the painting mood the colors would be vibrant and the strokes daring. She couldn't see a picture forming, just broad, forceful strokes. Bright orange, deep red, pitch black and muddy green. Each had a piece, each had a place. They floated about in her painter's vision with nowhere to land.

She marched down through the cramped corridor with ease, knowing most of the servants would be out and about within the house, so she had no fear of running into anyone. Finally, when she reached Charlotte's door, she set Lettie as look-out and Winnie would go in with her. Edwina was left behind in her room to stand sentry behind the locked door.

Chapter 21

"SHE'S NOT HERE, sir," the maid said, looking at Gabriel as if he'd missed something that everyone else knew.

"Do you know where she is?" He disregarded the girl and held his temper at his wife's absence yet again.

"Yes, I do. She chose to dine in the morning room this evening." Gabriel's brows furrowed as he turned toward the morning room.

Was that where she was rendezvousing with her secret lover? Gabriel mentally pommeled himself for leaping to the first conclusion that came to him. He tried to apply Bernard's suggestion in not assigning bad motives to Elizabeth, but it was easier said than done. It was the only thing he knew of human nature, to deceive and connive and defraud.

Gabriel admitted to knowing practically nothing of his wife's true character in such matters as confrontation. It was possible that she was running away from him, from the situation between them. He berated himself for acting so coarsely toward Elizabeth the night before and he was justly rewarded for his ill behavior, but he was in no mood for a cat and mouse caper. She would not run from him.

The butler was finishing his service to Elizabeth when Gabriel appeared unnoticed in the doorway of the morning room. Darwin placed before her broiled fish, creamed peas and bread pudding. It looked like a mountain of food considering her steady diet of soup as of late.

"Thank you, Darwin. You may return to the kitchen. My maids will be here with me if I'm in need of anything." She dismissed the elderly butler with a kind smile.

"One moment, please." Gabriel intercepted everyone's attention, startling Elizabeth most. "Please send a plate of whatever she is eating to me. I'll be sharing a meal with her tonight."

Elizabeth had to exert extreme effort to make her voice work properly. After hearing Gabriel's voice ring through the small room, resonating across every sore spot in her heart, then appearing in a royal blue doublet that accentuated the broadness of his shoulders and the narrowness of his waist. Elizabeth nearly cried.

"I must admit that I'm surprised you sought me out, let alone wish to dine with me," she said, hoping her voice was steady enough to not raise suspicion of her true emotions.

"Indeed," he offered without apology. Taking her hand and kissing its back, he could feel her pulse beating through her palm despite its coolness. He rubbed it in attempt to warm her, only to realize what her touch did to him.

Elizabeth had to force herself to breathe, and to keep her eyes from letting loose their floodgates. Her throat constricted painfully as she considered her predicament. The events surrounding her have been troublesome at best and would be easier to manipulate if he would take her away without reservation, but she knew that without solving the crimes cast upon her community there would be no hope of it. She withdrew her hand from his, not allowing him to linger so intimately with her.

Darwin delivered the requested plate after Gabriel seated himself opposite Elizabeth. Gabriel watched Elizabeth as she diverted her gaze. She paid more than the usual attention to her plate and settings, avoiding eye contact with him.

"Is there anything else you need, sir?" Darwin asked, placing the wine bottle to the side instead of attending them through the meal.

"Is there some rush, Darwin?" Gabriel was rather perturbed at the sloppy service he was receiving from the old man. Perhaps the household accepted it because of their long history, but it was approaching rudeness.

"No, sir, I'm just following household instructions, sir."

"And what instructions were those?"

"That I oversee the making of all consumables and serve the family personally, sir."

"Very well, thank you for being so conscientious. I'm sure protecting the family means a lot to you."

"It means everything, sir." Gabriel missed the direct eye contact between Darwin and Elizabeth.

"You have a very loyal staff," Gabriel said before taking his first bite of bland fish.

"Yes," she said, taking a bite herself, intentionally lingering over the small amount of flesh.

"Is the meal sitting well with you?" Gabriel wanted to engage Elizabeth into conversation, but felt at a loss.

"Yes, I do believe so." She was looking forward to richer, fully flavored food, but Marybeth urged her to be cautious and progress slowly. For the moment, though, the bland meal was the best she'd ever tasted. Elizabeth took another bite, noting Gabriel's intense attention to her every move.

"I'm wondering why you came down to the morning room to have dinner alone. I can only assume that you needed to escape your rooms."

All Elizabeth could do was nod her head in agreement. Pretending, deceiving, and defrauding took all her energy, all her joy, and robbed her of every element that meant happiness in her life. It was tiring. She had to seek refuge in a topic she didn't have to dance around.

"Have you visited your father yet?" she asked, upsetting his world in an instant.

"No, why do you ask?" Gabriel chocked out, not wanting to discuss his father, or any family for that matter.

"I haven't seen him in so long that I worry about him. He is surely worried since I haven't come for my routine visits. He agreed to allow me to paint his portrait and we were just discussing the details before being sent to Kathryn's aid," she said, unwilling to talk about the matter, "I want to put him at ease that I am recovering. I also want to tell him of our recent joining of families. He'll be most pleased," she said, trying to ignore the fact that she was causing Gabriel discomfort.

"You think he knows about what happened?" Gabriel asked, thinking that his father had sequestered himself from all reality with his hermetic lifestyle.

"Oh most definitely. I assure you that he knew shortly after. We are a close-knit community. Nothing much happens here without everyone knowing," she said, confident in the gossip mills to have borne the information quickly to her friend.

"Then surely he knows about our compulsory vows," he speculated aloud. She became quiet and reflective as she took her next bite and it set him to wondering. "Is it something I said?"

"No," she replied, not wanting to betray her thoughts. He didn't wish to be married. No wonder, she supposed. Having to endure such a scandal of divorced parents and to be robbed of your inheritance to boot would wound a young boy as evidence by the man she was married to. She didn't blame him for the reluctance to marry or the admission of such. Bernard was wrong in his assessment of Gabriel. It wasn't the long stint in the king's service, but deep-seated grievance of injustice that caused him such malcontent of others, especially women.

"Bernard came to me today," she said blandly.

"Bernard?" His response was somewhere between surprise and quizzical. "And what did you two have to talk about?"

"You."

"Cabrera." Bernard was conferring with several other men over the decision to move ahead to Piffenview without Gabriel when he heard the unmistakable voice of his commander.

"Yes sir."

"We need to talk," Gabriel said as he walked toward the opposite side of the courtyard. They ended up in an alcove along the south wall where only an aged dog lay to get out of the sun and take a mid-day snooze.

Bernard followed his chief and commander, knowing by the set of his jaw and the forcefulness of his gate that he'd learned of his visit with Elizabeth last afternoon. He braced himself for a tongue lashing for meddling in their private affairs.

"What did she say?" Gabriel's question took Bernard by surprise. Instead of a tirade of scolding, Gabriel sounded like a lovesick boy needing guidance with his first romantic interlude.

"She asked me if she hurt you." It took Gabriel a few seconds to absorb the weight of Bernard's words.

"Was that all?"

"Yes. I should tell you that I also informed her of your proclivity to ascribe impure motives and weak character to everyone around you."

"I know, she told me." Gabriel ran his hand through his hair and turned from his friend. "Truly, she didn't say anything else about me?"

"No, she only asked after your welfare, only concerned if she'd hurt you in any way. Did she seem all right last night?"

"Physically, she seems to be gaining her strength. She ate solid food, which pleased me immensely, but otherwise she's as uninterested and taciturn as ever."

"Yes, she's the same way with me. She seems to disconnect herself from the world quite often, closeting herself off. What do you think of that?" Bernard asked.

"I don't know her well enough to say that isn't her true personality."

"I suggest, then, that you talk with her more. Maybe you can surmise if there is a cause to her behavior or if it is her true nature."

"You think there is another element that I'm missing?"

"What I think is irrelevant. You have to make that judgment for yourself." Bernard offered, not knowing what else to say.

They returned to the crowded exercise yard, fully intending to carry on with their daily routine, when Gabriel noted a lone soldier making use of the water bucket. Not letting his men slack off their exercise routine, Gabriel set out to make an example of the missing soldier.

"Gaspar," Gabriel shouted over to the soldier taking his fill by the ladleful, "where is Durham?" The men were paired earlier and the other man was nowhere in sight.

"Inside. He's with Miss Elizabeth." Shock and curiosity shot through Gabriel and it showed on his face, not only for the activities of his wife but also for the informality in which the soldier addressed her. It spoke of impropriety yet resounded with familiarity. "She's requested several of us, one at a time, of course."

"What?" Gabriel couldn't comprehend Elizabeth's motives and asked after them.

"When I went in, it seems she just wanted company." Gaspar shrugged one shoulder to convey his lack noticing an apparent agenda on her part. "She had me sit with her as she did her needlepoint and had me tell her about myself and my family." The confounded look on Gabriel's face made Gaspar babble on as if to excuse them all of whatever sin they'd committed. "She doesn't keep us for long, a half an hour at the most then we return to the yard. It's all quite innocent, really."

This was ridiculous! Curiosity and complete bewilderment propelled Gabriel to search her out. He would get down to the bottom of this mess. He didn't have to travel far to find Elizabeth and Durham. She was in the receiving room, diligently sewing as Gasper had said, training her eyes on her work while Durham sat opposite her, grinned from ear to ear as he described his brood of children in great detail. Lilith was sitting across the room by the window reading a book, clearly disinterested in the conversation.

Gabriel cleared his throat to announce his arrival. Elizabeth looked up to see the gruff look on his face and instantly knew her time had been exhausted. She placed her needlepoint on the cushion beside her and made a gesture of a mildly concealed yawn.

"I thank you sincerely for sharing with me the antics of your children. It was truly delightful. Unfortunately, we'll have to continue another time, for I've depleted my energy for now," she consoled Durham.

"Of course," he said, standing to assist Elizabeth and placing her hand on his sleeve as he escorted her to her husband. "Another time then." He smiled down at her before giving a bow to his commander and heading back to the yard.

"Would you please escort me to my rooms?" she asked, managing another delicate yawn.

"Certainly," Gabriel vacillated between whether to ask her what she was up to or to leave it be. By the time they'd climbed the stairs and reached her door, he'd lost his chance. "I'm glad you were able to be out and about in the house today." He chose diplomacy rather than interrogation.

"Yes, it was nice, even if it was short lived."

"Until tonight then," he turned to her, hoping to see something, anything in her eyes that indicated her thoughts only to have her green eyes searching back. Raising both her hands and kissing her warm, porcelain skin Gabriel tried to gauge her reaction to his affections.

There was something unusual about Gabriel kissing the backs of her hands as he was. He lingered over them, stroked her palms with his fingertips, and pressed his warm, soft lips to her skin. Remembering their first kiss, Elizabeth's heart began to race and her breathing decidedly increased. Unaware of her physical reaction, she continued to stare into Gabriel's bold gaze and take in his presence. Wishing she could voice the stirrings he brought out in her, she knew this was not the time, nor were they formally wed. She restrained herself and waited for her day to come.

Unable to endure the agony, she withdrew her hands and bid him good day. Lettie opened the door when she'd heard Elizabeth's voice, timing it perfectly for her escape.

Gabriel stood in the hallway, feeling triumphant for seeing Elizabeth's reaction to him, knowing he could stir a palpable response from her. Her response to him was innate and uncontrived, he felt it in her pulse and saw it in her eyes. Her green eyes turned dark and were dripping with emotion, showing him what he wanted. Her outward façade could not hide her inward needs, her deep desire for him.

She pulled away from him and ran into her rooms. Her maid was there to deter him from running in after her, to delve deeper into her feelings for him. He found himself desperately needing clarity, explanation of her actions, her behavior, her mysterious nature. It festered in him long enough. He wanted answers. Gabriel found himself knocking on her door before he'd realized his intention.

"Yes, my lord," the maid answered.

"I need to speak with Elizabeth."

"I'm sorry, sir, but she has just laid down and asked that she not be disturbed."

"Fine. Tell her when she wakes that I'll be back at the customary time for dinner. If she chooses to go down to the morning room to dine again, please send for me and I'll escort her myself," he issued.

"Yes, my lord," closing the door and locking it, she turned back into the room to stoke the fire once more before her mistress fell asleep only to be interrupted by another knock.

"Why does Elizabeth have the door locked at all times?" Gabriel asked, perturbed at the constant barring from his wife.

"Why to keep others out my lord. She's done that as long as I've been with her."

Gabriel accepted the explanation and excused himself, apologizing for disturbing Elizabeth. He'd known people who needed a degree of autonomy that dictated they control their entire environment. It seemed Elizabeth was one of those people. He would delve deeper into that issue tonight. He could deal with that attribute much easier than if she were trying to deceive him deliberately.

Desperately wanting to deflect the destructive thought pattern emerging within him, he decided to distract himself with appreciating the art within the castle walls.

Chapter 22

"T HINGS ARE COMING *along nicely," he said, more to himself than to her.*
"How can you say that? Nothing is going as planned. Absolutely
nothing!" she protested, throwing her arms up in disbelief of his cool composure.

"Don't worry so much, my love. We have them running in circles, leaving
us time to execute our plan. They don't suspect a thing," he said with a satisfied
smile.

"I honestly don't share your vision. We surely can't move on to the next
phase as planned, not surrounded by Lord Athelston's men. How do you plan on
doing it?" she asked with baited breath.

"You'll see, my love. You'll just have to wait and see."

"Please, sir, please, you must come," a young maid pulled on Gabriel's
arm as soon as he entered the door and pled for his assistance. "He's
harassing her and won't leave her be," she cried in distress.

Indeed, Gabriel found a distressed Elizabeth detained in a chair by
Wesley. He'd been bending over her in a domineering manor and causing
angst as he smiled above her. Something protective gripped Gabriel unlike
anything he had ever experienced before.

"Elizabeth, may I be of assistance?" he asked in a menacing low
tone. She took a moment to compose herself before responding as Wesley
straightened himself.

"No," her response sounded forced and unnatural even to her own
ears.

"Then maybe I can be of assistance to Mr. Williams," Gabriel offered.

"Oh, no, I'm in no need of assistance. Thank you for your kind offer," he said, barely looking at the man twenty feet away giving him a look that would have made other men cower.

"I'm sure you don't see the need, but I assure you, Mr. Williams, that it is not a request. Please leave Miss Elizabeth's rooms," he said without doubt that he could forcibly remove the lad easily and without compunction.

Wesley, seemingly assessing his choices, reluctantly bid good day to Elizabeth and sailed out of the room, ignoring the speculative glare from the man he begged to go into battle with not long ago.

Elizabeth remained seated loosening the white-knuckled grip she had on her skirt.

"Elizabeth," Gabriel called to her. Stifling tears of frustration, she made no effort to get up. "Elizabeth, is there something amiss?"

"I have a headache. I've been up all morning and have probably over exerted myself." She avoided looking directly at him for fear of giving herself away, prompting more questions.

Something wasn't right, he thought. Elizabeth had been reclusive before, but she seemed downright despondent now. He went over to her and felt her forehead with his palm, an action almost to her undoing. The strain of concealing her emotions, sealing them away, made her nauseated.

"Open your eyes, Elizabeth." Gabriel's soft command was difficult for her to perform, knowing she couldn't hold back her tears if she did what she was told, but did it anyway. He was right above her, just as Wesley had been moments before. She couldn't help but look him in the eye. "We need to talk."

Helping her stand and leading her to the couch where he tenderly ministered to her needs, Gabriel carefully covered her shoulders with a shawl and ordered refreshments. He observed her movements, not pressuring her to talk until after her food was delivered. Her body language told its own story. She was withholding information she didn't want anyone else to know, but her eyes were the most telltale. They held consummate sadness.

"I know there is something going on," he said bluntly. She solidified his comment by being unsurprised by his statement and avoiding eye contact, paying more attention to the wrinkles in her skirt than him. "I'm not sure of what, but I plan on finding out." Reaction.

"Why?"

"Because it involves my wife. I'm going to find out why you are sneaking about the house just to see an injured servant when you aren't well yourself."

Gabriel hit a nerve. She was clearly agitated now, gripping the side of the couch, eyes as big as saucers. Whatever it was, she was neck deep in the middle of it, as well as emotionally involved. He could feel it to the bottom of his soul.

"How did you find out?" she said breathlessly.

"What interest do you have in a servant with a broken arm, beyond normal responsibility as mistress of the house?" he asked.

Elizabeth stood and began to wring her hands, formulating an answer she thought would appease him. How could she steer him astray, to not cause suspicion and raise alarm?

"Charlotte was my lady's maid for several years before the accident. I kept her up late the night she fell down the stairs, so I feel responsible, at least in part, for her injuries." She waited for Gabriel to indicate his acceptance of her story.

"Why did your maid insist that I come to your rescue just now?"

"I'm a very private person and need my space. She was helping me protect that."

"Why couldn't you just have told Wesley to go away?"

"He doesn't listen to me, besides, I'm not one for confrontation." She realized that her explanations were making her look weak, but she didn't care. As long as her explanations were plausible enough for him to believe and discontinue his query, she would remain weak in his eyes.

Gabriel remained seated, watching his wife lie through her teeth. She was as nervous as a blindfolded man about to face the gauntlet. She paced as she spewed her excuses, making them up as she went along. She couldn't look him in the eye and say those things. She had to place herself as far away as possible to avoid eye contact. No, lying wasn't her forte but she was unaware of how badly she practiced it and Gabriel wasn't about to inform her of his observation.

"Is that what you want me to believe? I think I should question her myself to get the real story." Elizabeth stood stock still before him. Plain, unadulterated fear covered her face.

"No, I can't allow you to do that. She's far too week and unable to stand agitation of any kind." Unable to fully expand her lungs from the constricting force of muscles around her rib cage, Elizabeth sat to keep herself upright. "Truly, I would appreciate it if you wouldn't trouble her. This is only a matter of the house, I swear."

His curiosity well beyond piqued, Gabriel was fully prepared to investigate this angle and what was behind Elizabeth's behavior. He wouldn't stop until he found the connection.

"Why was Wesley causing you grief?" he continued to Elizabeth's chagrin.

"Like I said, I have a headache and wanted to rest. Again, Wesley doesn't listen to me, so it was causing me a degree of anxiety to have him in my rooms," she spoke the truth, at least the part of causing her anxiety.

"Why did he insist on seeing you when he knew you were ill?" She was going to lie. She averted her eyes and fidgeted.

"Something only a younger brother would know. He's the only child of his mother and insists on getting his way, especially if it irritates another," she said, painting him as an annoying, immature sibling, which Gabriel didn't doubt.

"You would think a boy of his age would have outgrown that trait." He studied her movements. The topic of Wesley was most disconcerting to her. "What did he have to say that was so upsetting?" She closed her eyes, visibly controlling her emotions. She didn't speak for some time, giving rise to doubt that whatever she said was going to be truthful.

"He invited me down to dine with the family. He'd found that I had dined in the morning room with you last night, as a trial of my strength, and expressed the family's wishes for me to join them if I felt up to it." Yes, that sounded good to her ears. There was nothing to be misconstrued in her statement.

"Alright," he said after a prolonged silence, "I'm going to ask you one more question and I'll leave you to rest. I need you to be completely honest with me, Elizabeth. Look me in the eye," he ordered, she obeyed. Everything hinged on her answer, and he would know if she was lying to him. "Is there any reason why you wouldn't be able to be wed by the church?" he asked, ascertaining that she knew what he meant.

"No," she said adamantly. The look in her eyes told him the answer before she spoke the words. The denial came out in a forceful whisper, needing to escape. She hadn't realized she was crying until he handed her his handkerchief. She allowed him to guide her back to bed, pleased with how well the interview went. He bid her a good rest and departed.

She slept the remainder of the night to escape the torture. The maids turned away him away when he came to escort her to dinner, but he came into her bedroom, she supposed, to confirm she was indeed in bed and sleeping. She didn't fault him for that, but it didn't make her feel any less trapped.

Gabriel was disappointed when Elizabeth declined to dine with him that night, in her room or otherwise, claiming her headache kept her from having any appetite. His only chance to be with her alone was during their intimate dinners. He hadn't realized how much he'd looked forward to each bland meal until he was denied that privilege.

"I thought you had plans with Elizabeth?" Bernard said when Gabriel returned to the group of men eating stew from the pot in the middle of the camp.

"I did, she's not feeling well," he said, taking a seat beside his friend.

"Care for some stew?" Pecor offered.

"No, thank you. I eat with the family. It wouldn't be good manners to show up to the dinner table full, now would it?"

"Maybe not, but it would be a lot less stodgy," Higgins blurted out, not thinking that his commander was one of 'them'.

After the men finished and began to doze off, Bernard took this chance to talk with Gabriel.

"I've been thinking," he started, unsure of how his friend would accept his suggestion. "You said that Elizabeth was uninterested and taciturn as of late. Have you really tried to talk with her?" He asked, gaining him a look that bespoke ire and frustration. "What do you talk about?"

"It isn't as social as you would like, I'm sure," he admitted. Bernard immediately rolled his eyes. "I'm boring, is that it?"

"No. Maybe. Ok, yes. If you don't know how to talk to a woman to gain her interest, then you aren't going to get very far. And before you say that you've talked with plenty of women before, I tell you that you haven't. Not really. The women at court are self-absorbed and single minded. Elizabeth is different."

"And how do you know this?" Gabriel asked, interested in his friend's observation.

"Just by looking at her, Gabriel, she isn't the frilly, bejeweled, self-centered type of woman, neither is she the fragile, helpless type. She's an intellectual," Bernard said, liking the way it fit.

"And how did you come to this conclusion?"

"Have you ever looked at the books on her bedside table? She's reading Julian of Norwich's "Showings of Divine Love". This is a book of intellectuals. Also, she paints wonderful pictures, another sign of intellectualism." Bernard could see Gabriel grasping his point. "And in light of that, I think it will take a little more than small talk to get her to open up to you."

"Do you have any suggestions, oh wise one?" Gabriel mocked, secretly holding in his hope of gaining his wife's love and attention.

"You have something that she would find ultimately interesting." Bernard suggested, not mentioning what that thing was in mixed company as they were, sleeping or not.

Gabriel sat back and thought, wondering if she would receive it well. He wasn't about to reveal his secret to someone he couldn't trust, even if that person was his wife. But, deep down, he knew he could trust her. He wanted to with all his heart. He needed to for the sake of his purpose in life, his future happiness. Bernard left Gabriel to mull over the decision to share his most prized secret with someone he was not sure he was willing to trust.

Chapter 23

D INNER WITH THE family was once again quiet and uneventful. Gabriel was caught up in his own thoughts and plans and paid little attention to the others at the table. Having felt he was complete with his duties in participating in dinner, Gabriel excused himself. Reflective in the way dinner was carried out, Gabriel could understand where Elizabeth could take on the environment set around her. It was sedate to say the least.

Back in his rooms, he let Bernard's words ring through his thoughts, seriously considering taking his suggestion and putting it into action. Tonight. It had been several hours since he'd last checked in on Elizabeth and maybe she was up for receiving visitors.

In a burst of optimism, Gabriel decided to do it before he lost his nerve. He took out a book from his trunk and knew he had to keep it hidden from sight. He removed the pillow from its slip and placed the book within it. Thinking fast, he took the sash from the curtain and tied it about the book, effectively making it look like a gift.

Feeling as if he were delivering vital information, Gabriel traversed the hallways, looking out for any passers-by. Lilith and Wesley were downstairs, he could hear them talking. They were getting closer. He would have to hurry. Fortunately for him, Edwina was returning from an errand and she let him into the room unnoticed, locking the door behind her.

"Is she awake?" he whispered, not wanting to disturb Elizabeth if she were still under the weather.

"Yes, just so. I'll ask if she will receive you, my lord." Gabriel heard whispers, but no one materialized until sometime later, after Elizabeth was made presentable.

"Good evening, Gabriel." She'd sat up in bed, propped by pillows. Even in this state, she didn't seem frail or helpless. She indeed did have the book of a female philosopher on her night stand. Bernard was proving to be more astute than Gabriel gave him credit for. Unfortunately, the stoic nature remained.

"Good evening." Gabriel instantly felt nervous as he held the heavy book in his grasp. What if she rejected him and what he believed? Donning an imaginary coat of arms, he pressed forward, not shrinking back from what hadn't yet happened. "Please, may we have some privacy?" Gabriel asked. Elizabeth motioned for all three maids to leave them.

"You have something for me?" She asked when he apparently seemed stuck on his words, noticing the crudely wrapped parcel in his hands.

"Yes." Taking a step farther into the room, Gabriel began to have second thoughts about confessing to her, but his mission prevailed. "I want to share something with you." He looked over his shoulder to ensure they were alone and unattended. "I hope you will appreciate its value." He placed the heavy parcel on her lap and waited with great anticipation as she unwrapped it.

"I like what you've done with the window sash," she chided. He smiled back at her nervously. She unwound the sash and peeled the pillow slip away to reveal the brown leather of a new book. It didn't have an embossed cover, so she hefted it and read the spine. A sharp gasp of breath and an astonished look at Gabriel brought him to sit on the bed beside her.

The spine read "The Whole Bible" written by Coverdale. It was the first of its kind, being written in English. Elizabeth knew that people were martyred as heretics for owning such a book, and Gabriel was walking around with it in her home!

"Gabriel Anderson Athelston, do you know how much trouble you could be in owning this?" Despite her objections, Gabriel was pleased to find her opening it, scanning its pages, mesmerized by its pictures.

"Not according to the king. Since he fell out of the good graces with Rome, he's given license to Coverdale. This copy was given to me by his Majesty himself." Not misinterpreting her interest, he watched her in fascination as she became engrossed with the book. "But I know some that

I come across will still be stuck in the old times and would take exception to my having it. I would hate for it to fall into the wrong hands. There are plenty of people who would prefer to throw it into the fire than read it."

"Oh, not me," she said, unaware of the open glimpse she was giving Gabriel. "I would treasure it."

"As do I," Gabriel delighted, finding himself smiling, immensely relieved that she didn't scorn him for having such a book. "I must admit that it's been somewhat of a boon for me. It helps me keep my mind about me as well as centering me through troubled times."

Elizabeth looked away from the book and fixed her attention on Gabriel. "What kind of troubled times?" she asked, seemingly more interested in him than ever before.

"In my line of work, with the people I deal with every day, moral dilemmas come up quite often. Reading the Bible keeps me grounded, and helps me realize that, although we are human, there is a Greater One that sees everything, knows everything and one day He is going to get rid of all that is bad." He paused, drinking in the sight of her in her shift, her hair barely bridled and her cheeks flushed. He ached to hold her, to caress her, to press her against the pillows behind her. "And, when I make mistakes, it helps me with that too."

"What kind of mistakes?" she asked, unable to think of anything else to say while he was looking at her that way. He was staring at her lips while she spoke.

Forgetting that she just asked him a question, Gabriel acted on his need to touch her. He pressed his palm to her warm, soft cheek only to have her snuggle into it, breathing in the smell of him. She reached up and covered his hand with hers, placing the other over his heart. It was too much for Gabriel. Sliding his fingers into her silky brown hair, he brought her to him, to meet his lips.

He pressed his lips to hers in a joyous riot of emotion and exhilaration. Her soft lips molded to his, bringing a deep sigh of relief as she relaxed. With eyes closed and a willing spirit, she allowed herself to imbibe, allowed herself to enjoy.

He kissed her over and over, teasing her lips, gliding over them in luscious form. Plucking at them, sucking on them, using his tongue. Despite the odd sensations she felt, she allowed Gabriel to administer these wonderful feelings as he pleased. The first kiss they shared was just as brief and fleeting as the second. This one, though, she would always remember.

Gabriel brought himself closer to her inch by inch, shoving the heavy, cumbersome book aside to facilitate his goal. He then took both her arms, placing them around his neck, allowing him to wrap his arms around her, pressing her body to his. Her thin shift drove him next to insanity. He wanted her in the worst way.

Elizabeth reveled in the sensations Gabriel was giving her. Allowing herself to be swept away in his arms, she found the needed retreat her life called for, the sanctuary she sought. She clung to it as hard as she could. Swimming in it, drowning her fears and sorrows, Elizabeth reciprocated Gabriel's affection.

Gabriel wanted, no, needed to deepen the kiss. His desire pushed past all else in his brain to land on the knowledge that she was his wife, his for the taking. There wasn't anything stopping him. He could care less about the three maids in the next room, he needed to be with Elizabeth.

Coaxing Elizabeth to open for him was both a challenge and a joy. She pulled away from him at first, not knowing what to think, then tentatively allowed him to show her how beautifully sensual this type of kissing could be. He felt her relax and give him control. He wanted more, needed more, advancing slowly for her benefit as well as his own. Enfolding her face between his palms, he tilted her head to one side and pushed her chin down with his thumb and began exploring deeper, penetrating her mouth with his tongue.

Elizabeth wasn't ready. She jumped out of his tender embrace and scoured him with critical eyes. Chest heaving with exertion, pulse pounding furiously, she scathed his advances.

"I don't-I can't-what was-?" she asked, covering her mouth with a feminine hand, unable to put a whole sentence together to save her life.

"I'm sorry I should have waited until you were fully recovered. I didn't mean for it to go so far, but I couldn't help myself," he said, just as out of breath as she. Gabriel suffered greatly from the abrupt separation but remained seated beside her, reveling in her reaction to him. "I'm sorry if I scared you." Commingling emotions both elated and disappointed Gabriel. He knew without a doubt that Elizabeth hadn't experienced kissing as he was demonstrating, leading him to the triumphant feeling that she was still untouched by another. He was eternally grateful for that knowledge, but also disappointed for the abrupt separation from her sweetness. Her wide, bewildered eyes stared back at him as if to ask what he'd just done to her and examining her own emotions about the exchange.

"I don't know what I feel, but I'm not scared. It was just so foreign."

"My dear," Gabriel smiled a rather satisfied smile, "when you figure it out, I'll be nearby." He knew that being close to her would only fare badly in her condition, so he took his leave. "Good night," he placed a kiss on her forehead, "sleep tight," and one on her nose, "don't let the bed bugs bite," finally placing another lingering kiss on her softened lips.

She wasn't sure when she realized he'd left the Coverdale with her, but she didn't want to chance anyone finding it. Feeling strangely honored that he had left it in her care, she quickly replaced it into the pillow slip and put it under the covers with her. She slept with it, keeping it close to her heart for as long as she could.

Gabriel lay in bed that night replaying the scenario in his mind. What was so different about her tonight? She wasn't withdrawn or uncommunicative, she responded to him as he never would have expected. Had he taken her off her guard by gaining her intrigue with the Coverdale? Was her sullenness a facade? Thinking of the numerous possibilities that lay between them, he wished he could carry her far away from here and discover her away from this place, one on one. How would she act away from all the entrapments she surrounded herself with, on her own without her safeguards? Allowing her to hole herself up in her rooms was only facilitating peccant habits. He would have to work extra hard to draw her out. He relished the thought of drawing her out in private, envisioning peeling away her layers of complexity along with her clothes. He fell asleep with that last thought in his head.

Chapter 24

THE NEXT MORNING, things were looking up for Elizabeth. Despite having plenty of rest, she knew that her energy reserves wouldn't withstand anything vigorous. She opted for watching others ride their horses, work within the gardens, busy themselves at their business. Sitting on the second floor balcony on this clear, bright day allowed her to take in as much as she could bear.

Unable to control the itch to walk, even if it were a short distance, Elizabeth decided to walk along the castle walls. There were plenty of places to take a rest if she became too fatigued. She so loved Listhenshire and feared it had somehow changed since she'd been indisposed. She needed to see that it remained the same, whole and unchanged, as the steadfast beauty it was.

"Is Gabriel here?" she asked a handsome young man watching over two men fighting with wooden swords.

"No, he and some of his men went hunting. Allow me to introduce myself," he said with a bow, "I'm Justin Pecor." Elizabeth thought he looked awfully young to be a soldier. His height, though, opposed the young face aiding her to judge him to be in his early twenties.

"I'm pleased to meet you, Justin." She gave him a stately bow. "Would you be so kind as to accompany me with a turn about the wall?"

"It would be my pleasure." He flashed a grin and offered her his arm. "It's a fine day you chose to take a walk, Mrs. Athelston."

"Yes, I believe it is." Inhaling the fresh air deeply into her lungs, Elizabeth felt like a year of rust fell from her. Her muscles felt as if they were missing their usefulness. "I like to see the keep so busy. Of course, I haven't ever seen it this busy, but busy nonetheless."

"It is a beautiful area. You were fortunate to grow up here." They rounded the first corner, placing them fully in the sun. She let it warm her skin.

"Yes, I believe so." Noticing even more men practicing their fighting skills with wooden swords, Elizabeth asked Justin about it.

"We stay in fighting form when we keep up our skills. Most of us are going to Piffenview shortly to replace Lord Garrott's legion. We'll be fending off the Scots from invading that border. That takes skill and practice."

"I see." She pondered what he'd said for a moment before asking, "Will Gabriel be going with you?"

"No, he is sending a select group. You are slowing your pace, My Lady. Why don't you take a rest before going any further." He guided her to the marble bench beside some rosebushes and seated her before seating himself. To fill the time while she rested, Justin pointed out several of the men and stated their names. He explained their fighting techniques and the reasons behind each move.

"I'm sorry I'm probably boring you to death."

"Quite the contrary. I never knew the first thing about sword fighting. It's not likely that I'll take it up, but it is interesting."

They were having a good time with enough repartee to fill in the time spent on the bench when Justin was called away. Another man, Douglas Manchester, replaced him. It was quite nice to have so many distractions about her. Douglas walked her around another corner and enticed her into walking farther into camp. Once there, she was perched upon a wooden stool while watching the comings and goings of the people that were now her people, her husband's people.

She talked with the wives of the men, some with children and some without. They talked about the journey here and how far they plan on traveling before reaching their destination. She met children of all ages, dogs of all breeds, and ate stew cooked over an open pit. It was splendid.

"What is she doing?" Gabriel asked Bernard, noticing his wife sitting smack dab in the middle of the camp as if she belonged there. They stood side by side, arms folded against their chest watching her endear herself to the people.

"She's making friends, I believe. After all, she will be the lady of the manner. It will suit her to be approachable and liked by the people."

Elizabeth stayed out in the yard with the common folk and soldiers all morning and part of the afternoon. She was having so much fun that she didn't want to leave, but leave she must. "I feel so much better today. I think I'll take a rest and join the family for dinner tonight," she said, allowing Gabriel to escort her back into the house.

"You must be careful, Elizabeth," the statement came from behind them, seemingly appearing from nowhere. Lilith stood not ten yards away from them looking pouty and concerned. "You don't want to wear yourself out. The last thing you need is to catch your death before Gabriel can take you away."

Gabriel escorted Elizabeth to her rooms and waited until she was safely behind the door and heard the usual lock put in place before heading down the stairs.

"If you'll be so kind as to join us in Edward's study, Lord Athelston," Lilith said as she led the way.

Gabriel had no greater foreboding feeling than when he followed Lilith into the study and found Edward's sullen, if not slacken, unsmiling face greet him along with Wesley, who was unusually skittish.

"Thank you for coming, Lord Athelston," Edward said before sitting in his chair with a vessel full of port before him and took a healthy guzzle.

"May I ask what the matter of discussion is to be?" he asked, wondering about the delay to bring matters forth.

"Please, sit before we talk," Lilith offered, taking over the conversation. "We need to discuss matters of the wedding."

"I gave you two weeks in which to be prepared. In two days' time we will be wed. I will not waiver," he said firmly.

"You might change your mind after our discussion, Lord Athelston. Please, sit and let us talk," Lilith patted the seat next to her on the couch.

"Be on with it," he said, refusing Lilith in irritation of family demands. He became annoyed at the crassness Edward was showing, drowning his sorrows of losing a daughter to a husband while setting his wife to appeal their plea, incorporating the presence of her son for added family pressure. He wasn't going to be swayed.

"We ask for your sympathy and your sense of mercy," Lilith beseeched.

"For Christ's sake, you think I was going to kill the girl, not marry her. You will see her again, I assure you," he impatiently huffed, turning toward the door in response to their ploy.

"You have to get an annulment," Wesley stated boldly.

Gabriel turned in surprise. Wesley had come forward after making the unprecedented statement. Standing stock still while Gabriel approached him with disdain, Wesley burst forth with his confession.

Elizabeth couldn't resist the pull of the sun's warmth. She stepped out onto the grand balcony overlooking the gardens. Instead of casting her eyes on its beauty, she closed her eyes and tilted her chin up toward the sky to let the sun caress her, warm her, bathe in its glow. She smiled as she recalled Gabriel's tender touch. It robbed her of her sleep, keeping her awake with promise.

Soon she would be away from here, on her way to Piffenview with her new husband. She dreamed about it every night since he described it to her. She dreamed about the land, the people, the castle, and most of all, its lord. Yes, she would be leaving behind many things she cherished, but she was looking forward to her new life.

"Thinking of your lover?" Gabriel's voice came from behind her, startling her blissful reverie.

"Excuse me?" she asked, curious of his query and his tone. Being blinded by the sunlight, she stepped closer to him and let her eyes adjust, only to find him looking quite disturbed.

"Don't trifle with me, Elizabeth. Tell me now, do you have a lover?" he ground out.

"No," she gasped her denial.

In full disbelief of his bride, Gabriel took her by the wrist and pulled her through the corridor and into her rooms, decidedly showing her to her bedchamber.

"What are you to do, Lord Athelston?"

"I'm taking advantage of my rights as husband. Undress yourself or I shall," he said, clearly indicating his intention to follow through with the threat by pulling off his tunic and brandishing his well-muscled torso. "I can see your dismay. Might I ask what is in the way?"

"In the eyes of the church, we are not man and wife," she said, concerned for the rightness of the situation.

Gabriel wasn't in the mood to discuss anything. He was tired of lying, cheating women who would do anything to get what they wanted. Seeing that she wasn't complying with his command to disrobe he abandoned his own disrobing to take hold of her and gave her relief while unbuttoning the back of her dress.

"King Henry thinks he owns the church, so they will not question it. Before God and man, we were man and wife as soon as he signed the paper, that is unless you have a reason to object," he said.

"As much as I think I might enjoy it," she admitted, being seduced by his bare chest under her palms, "I regretfully ask for concession."

"And what concession would that be?" Finally at the last button, Gabriel was finally able to pull her dress down to bare her beautiful shoulders.

"If we could wait for the nuptials and-" she couldn't think straight as he began kissing her neck and shoulder.

"And what?" he said, trying not to like her response to his caresses.

"And-and a bedding party," she said, shaking with delight even when he abruptly stopped.

"What?" he asked in disbelief.

"It is something that I have just recently resolved to do."

"I don't understand. You are so private that your maids tell me you won't even allow them in the room when you bathe. What would make you subject yourself to a bedding party?" he asked.

"I have it on good authority that chastity is a rarity. I guess that it is just my nature. I don't want to be seen as like all the others," she said quite uncomfortably.

"All the other what?" he asked.

"I've been told that it is common for everyone, even females, of a certain age to dally. Regardless of that belief, I have been raised otherwise. That is why I ask for the bedding party, as proof that I am pure and have not offended God's law," she said with all sincerity.

Gabriel dropped his hands and backed away from her. He couldn't make up his mind if this was a trick, a cruel trick that would trap him into being stuck with a conniving liar for the rest of his life, or something much more complex.

Elizabeth was puzzled. She knew that Gabriel was an unpredictable man, but his mood swings were worrisome. She stayed quiet as he paced, running his hand through his hair, shaking his head and talking to himself. Really, there was no understanding the man.

"Please, tell me what is upsetting you," she said softly, hoping to gain insight to this man's thinking.

"I need to think. I'm too close to the matter. Who is telling the truth?" he said to himself.

"The truth about what?" she asked, pulling her dress to right and attempting to button it.

"If I believe you, give you the nuptials you want and the bedding party you crave and find out that you have tricked me, I shall be trapped. Everyone will know that I married and bedded someone that has been unfaithful and there is no recourse, no annulment can be had. On the other hand, if they are lying, what is their gain?"

"I don't understand. Has someone said that I have not been faithful?" she asked, bringing Gabriel to a halt. Was she as innocent as she looked?

"Your family just informed me that we needed to petition for annulment because you and Wesley are lovers."

There was nothing Elizabeth could say. There was nothing that came to mind. Her entire body shook with shock as she took in the accusation. Tears sprang as hatred for Wesley and his despicable mother crept into the pit of her stomach. How dare they, how dare they besmirch her name and her chances of happiness, her life?

Gabriel knew the answer. Elizabeth was not to blame. She had a lot to lose, but none more than her family. The motive may be their own selfishness, but it would be at the cost of the woman they wanted to keep for themselves for whatever reason. He faced Elizabeth, forcing her to look at him.

"Tell me," he whispered, placing a tender kiss on her down-turned lips. "Tell me what makes you cry so. Tell me why they would say such a thing."

Chapter 25

"YESTERDAY, WHEN YOU asked me why Wesley wouldn't leave me alone, I told you that he always insists on getting what he wants. Well, it seems his mother feels the same way. Whatever Wesley wants, he gets. Wesley has been pursuing me since the moment he arrived, so much so that he nearly accosted me in this very room. If it hadn't been for my lady's maid, Charlotte, he may have succeeded."

"Does that explain her condition?"

"Yes, that is my belief, but I cannot prove it. She won't even confess it to me."

"What was the real reason Wesley was here yesterday?" he asked. He noted her reluctance to answer.

"I know I should have confided in you sooner, but Wesley was too swift. I received a letter from his head master in direct response to a letter I had written to one of his professors." Elizabeth emptied the trunk at the foot of her bed to open the false bottom and produce the missive. "He was threatening me when you arrived, that if I showed this to anyone I would be sorry."

Gabriel opened it and began reading, understanding why Wesley wouldn't want this to come to light.

Dear Miss Hollingberry,

My name is Allen Horner and I am Head Master at Cambridge University. I'm sure you weren't expecting me to write you, but I am responding to your letter you wrote Professor Deventer on his behalf. Unfortunately, Professor Deventer couldn't respond to your request at the time of the receipt of your letter, for he was ill. Since then he has met an untimely demise and I have taken it upon myself to respond to you. Besides, Professor Deventer and Mr. Williams were not on the best of terms after Wesley was threatened with expulsion for allegedly cheating on an exam. Wesley was exonerated from the charge, of course, but the chance of getting a favorable response from the late professor would have been slim to nil.

I'm aware that Wesley Williams has already been received home by now, but if you are still inclined to know, I will tell you what you wish. From what I know of him, Wesley was a studious fellow with great ambition. He wasn't the most popular boy, favoring to be on his own or devoting himself to his studies. I don't know him personally, but from his transcripts, I can see he held good marks. He excelled in alchemy and took many classes in that field, opting to work with his instructors after hours and taking extra assignments that interested him.

Beyond the required education, Wesley selected archery and fencing as electives. He has good marks with many notes from the instructors of his talent and skill. He competed in, and won, last year's fencing championship, awarding him with a medal and his name on our plaque of yearly champions. We are very proud of him.

As to a suggestion for a gift for the boy, I couldn't suppose one way or another since I don't know him. My parents gave me a compass and it has served me well.

I hope this letter helps you in your endeavor to know a little more about your brother, but only time will remedy that malady.

Sincerely,
Allen Horner, Head Master

"Good. Excellent even. This helps in my investigation," he said with a smile. Noting Elizabeth's understandably battered spirit Gabriel gathered her up into his arms and kissed her soundly. "Don't worry, I'll protect you. Better yet, I'll make it up to you tonight, but first I have some business to attend to."

"Be careful," she said, not wanting to think any more on the matter and trusting that he will take her away soon and all of this will be behind her.

"I will. Do you smell smoke?"

No sooner had his senses picked up the scent of smoke than the call rang out for water. They scrambled to see what was set ablaze. To her horror, Elizabeth knew as soon as she detected the acrid stench that it was her painting barn. Billows of dark smoke marked the sky as it drifted above her precious place of solace, penance for telling the truth.

"I'm sorry, Elizabeth," said a familiar voice behind her, one she wished hadn't hurt so when he spoke her name. She turned to him with his reddened face streaked with tears of regret, remorse and pain of loss.

"Why, Papa, why?" she asked, but couldn't bring herself to stay for the answer. She needed an escape. She needed to get away. Thinking only of running, she mounted Majesty and pushed her as fast as she would go.

It took several hours before the fire was doused, having pushed the men back with its acrid, black smoke that impeded pressing forward from any direction. The battle made Gabriel all that much more irritable having to delay addressing the foremost matter in his mind.

Finally, when the flames were under control, Gabriel was finally able to campaign for the truth. The blaze was started in the center of the barn with all of the canvases, oily rags and more than enough paint to give the pile a long burn time. It didn't fall in line with the other acts of vandalism. He immediately looked toward the house where he knew the answers lay.

"Bring me the family. We have things to discuss," Gabriel ground out.

"Lord and Lady Hollingberry are in the study, sir. Wesley and Elizabeth are not here," said the soldier, unaware of the profound affect those words would have on his commander.

"Where are they?" he asked, already heading for his stead.

"I don't know where Wesley is, but Elizabeth rode off in that direction shortly after the fire was discovered," he replied, pointing in the direction Gabriel could only hope meant she found sanctuary.

"Find Wesley," he commanded gruffly before urging his stead to a full run.

Laughtonwood. Standing at a distance, even in the fading light of day, the gardens, the castle, the forest lining the grounds, it all looked exactly the same as the day he left. Remembering the day he'd looked back at his only home and vowed that he would never return, he recalled the feeling of absolute loneliness and consummate sadness at the lives lost within the walls he left behind. Although the people were still alive, in many ways they were all dead.

Gabriel pressed onward, steeling himself for the bitter cold reception he expected from his father. Elizabeth painted a different picture of him as of late, but Gabriel couldn't fathom a man who was attentive to another's needs, let alone be concerned over their well-being as she'd intimated. No, his father was cold and heartless, preferring to closet himself from everyone and everything over the heartache caused by a woman. The man Elizabeth spoke of could not have been the same man.

Still, Gabriel held his breath as he followed the young butler to the back room, his father's private rooms, where he found his wife.

It was not the scene he'd envisioned. Lincoln was sitting in a high-backed chair with blankets surrounding him while Elizabeth sat on the floor with her legs beneath her and taking in the fire's warmth. Her arms were draped across Lincoln's lap, holding the book she was reading aloud to him. Gabriel was sure his father was fast asleep. Gabriel gazed upon them unnoticed.

Even with the fire, Gabriel could see the frightening shade of yellow his father's tone had taken. Despite his natural thinness, whatever was causing his father's illness had also taken a good amount of weight from him.

Elizabeth was carefully fussing over him, making sure he was securely covered and comfortable when she noticed Gabriel standing just inside the shadows. Not wanting to disturb Lincoln, Elizabeth urged Gabriel into the hallway.

"He needs his rest. Please, announce yourself later," she pleaded.

"Is he dying?" he found himself asking.

"I don't know. It was quite an abrupt onset of symptoms, but he won't allow a physician to examine him," she said, stifling tears of anticipatory grief.

"He has always been stubborn like that. He pushes everyone away, even if it puts him at a disadvantage."

"No not this time. I know what you mean and, yes, I saw that part of him too, but this is different."

"How can this be different, and how can you assume you know anything about him? You weren't even born when my mother left us," he said defensively, feeling the intense need to leave this place once more and take his naive bride with him.

"Because I've observed him, I've talked with him, and I have come to understand him. I've come to understand that he loves and cares deeply and that was his downfall," she said, with empathy in her voice and on her face.

"I beg to differ," he said, gripping her upper arms in effort to make her understand, "after my mother left, leaving us in the worst way possible, ashamed and destitute, he pushed everyone away, include his own children. Yes he loves and cares deeply, but it is only himself in which you can apply those attributes."

"No, if you will just talk with him, get reacquainted with him, you will find that he does care for all those around him, so much so that it scares him. He hides from it out of self-preservation."

"I don't wish to be acquainted with a man who hides from those he loves. He's ruined himself over a woman, and he's ruined the rest of his family because of it."

"You're right," Lincoln said.

Gabriel's countenance hardened as if bracing for a blow. With all of the fortitude and strength he'd been trained with, he faced his father with hardened features and feigned disinterest.

"It's good to see you again, Gabriel. You've changed," Lincoln said with a surprisingly strong voice despite his feeble appearance.

"It seems as I am the only one." There was no malice in Gabriel's tone, but his eyes conveyed his true feelings.

"You've grown into a fine young man, despite your upbringing. I feel sorry for the circumstances that made our lives so different, so difficult to live past," Lincoln said.

"Speak for yourself. I do not hide myself from the world," Gabriel fired back, not wanting to compare himself to his father.

"Examine yourself, Gabriel. You will find that you have been affected too."

Gabriel's brows furrowed with frustration before he quit the conversation by way of silence. He wasn't going to fall victim to his father's way of thinking.

"There's no choice but to accept the truth, Gabriel. All you have to do is open your eyes and see it for what it is," Lincoln stated as a matter of truth to Gabriel's stoic face. "That is why you haven't taken your wife."

Gabriel's heart turned cold as his accusing eyes fell on Elizabeth. She betrayed a confidence to a man that would ultimately use as a weapon. He should have expected it, rather than be blindsided by it as he was now. His father had intercepted his wife's heart before he even had a chance.

"Stop it, you two. I can't stand for this bickering. Lincoln, why would you say such a thing?" Elizabeth asked.

"Because, my dear, when you first told me that you and Gabriel had been wedded by the king and for two weeks had been under the same roof, I knew you hadn't been bedded. You don't speak of him as a woman who'd been loved. No, you are the same as before, innocent and untouched, bringing me to the conclusion that a virile young man, such as your husband, has unresolved issues keeping him from performing what most men would take at a moment's notice with a beautiful woman such as yourself."

"I do not have unresolved issues keeping me from bedding my wife," Gabriel growled, "I made a promise to her step-mother that I wouldn't take her before she was fully recovered from her injuries."

Elizabeth could not hold back a gasp of surprise. In attempt to hide her growing ire, she went back to the fire, warming herself from the abrupt coolness she felt, feeling chilled to the bone.

Gabriel followed her without hesitation. Something had shaken her so much that she was trembling with it. He wrapped his arms around her trembling form liking the feeling of her there. His chin rested comfortably on the top of her head as she stared into the fire.

"Please don't disengage yourself again. Tell me what upsets you so about Lilith wanting to protect you?" he asked mistakenly.

"She wasn't protecting me, my lord. She was staving you off to give Wesley more time, time that he wasn't able to use."

"I don't understand."

"Of course you don't because I didn't tell you," she said, separating herself from his tender embrace. "I didn't mean to do any more than spare my family shame, but all I did was subject it to pain and suffering." Elizabeth didn't look back at Gabriel for fear distrust and accusation would be her mirror.

"I knew it," Lincoln burst forth with renewed vigor. "The day you came to ask me to be your next portrait you were different. Every time I mentioned Wesley's name you cringed. What has he done?"

"He couldn't fulfill his mission so he recruited his mother. The day after he accosted me I approached Lilith with the intent to stop things in their tracks only to have the tables turned on me. She told me that I was to be appreciative of his advances and she encouraged me to sleep with him," she confessed, unable to look at either man. "With her request, she bought him more time to make their lie believable."

"That you and he are clandestine lovers?" Gabriel recalled every last detail of that lie and the turn it took, nearly ending with forcing himself on his innocent bride. It would have not been the bedding she deserved. Had he followed through with it he would have found her still a virgin after Wesley's lie, hence, the distraction of the fire with Wesley's subsequent disappearance sparing him the wrath he fully deserved. Gabriel took Elizabeth into his arms once more, giving her trembling body support.

"There were so many times I thought you might come to me, but you stopped yourself. I thought you didn't want me," she confessed.

Gabriel turned Elizabeth around and brought her to face him. Tears lingered in her eyes as he placed gentle kisses on her lips. Had they been alone, he would have demonstrated more affection to show her how he truly felt.

"Shame or no, they need to be stopped. I'm going to send for my men. I'll be back in a minute," Gabriel said, making quick strides toward his horse. "Go get Bernard, Agrippa," he commanded his horse before giving him a sound slap on his rump, sending the faithful stead on the errand. He found himself wanting, even yearning to return to Elizabeth's side in order to get to know her more without prejudice of mind.

Lincoln and Elizabeth were being lead to the dining room when he returned. Just as they were being served, an earth-shattering explosion rocked the foundation. After making sure the others were uninjured, Gabriel set off to find its source.

Chapter 26

ELIZABETH WOKE WITH a splitting headache. The last thing she recalled was watching Gabriel run from the dining hall when she felt something hard hit the back of her head and everything went black.

There was nothing that could explain her predicament. She was bound to a chair in an unfamiliar dark room. She heard water dripping from a distance, echoing eerily and a damp chill filled the air. Without light she could only imagine that she was in a cavern but couldn't fathom where in Suffolk a cavern would be.

Suddenly she heard a noise beside her. It sounded like grunting. She waited breathlessly to hear it again to determine its origin. She wasn't alone.

"Lincoln, are you there?" she whispered.

"No, he's on the other side of you, still passed out if I had to guess."

"Wesley?" she asked, bewildered at the revelation.

"Yes, they got me too. I'm trying to get free of these ropes before they come back," he said, grunting and trying to pry his hands loose.

"Who did this?" she asked.

"I don't know. We didn't exchange formal introductions," he said sardonically.

Elizabeth began working on her bindings as well. Whoever tied her was very knowledgeable of knotting for she could barely begin to figure out how to wriggle free from the ornate scheme of rope about her wrists that were tied behind her back. Perhaps if she could see it she may be able to figure it out, but that wasn't an option.

"Don't fuss too much with your bindings, children. If they find you had loosened them they are likely to make them tighter and less escapable," Lincoln's feeble voice cut through the darkness. He sounded weaker than before making Elizabeth worry for his delicate condition.

"Sir Athelston, are you all right?" she asked.

"Yes, my dear, I am all right. Beware, Elizabeth. Protect yourself," he said noting the light heading their way.

Three figures appeared but only one was carrying a lamp. They were indeed in a cavern, as the light came closer throwing shadows over the uneven walls and ceiling. This was not a natural cavern as Elizabeth had imagined. It was a mine shaft.

Elizabeth concentrated on the only soul she could see. She recognized him instantly. He was Thomas Guiford, the smithy that worked for them. Troubled and confused, she looked at him with disheartened shock at his treasonous action against her and her family. He stood before them unabashedly, preferring to remain silent as he held the lamp high with one arm while the other was suspended in a sling.

Next to come into view was Lincoln's butler, which was no surprise. He was the only one who could have delivered the blow to the back of her head. He wasted no time in checking their bindings. Satisfied that they were still in place, he returned to stand beside his cohort.

"Mark, why are you doing this? Haven't I been kind to you after all these years?" Lincoln asked the butler. His plight fell on deaf ears.

"Everyone is secure," he said to the third person still cloaked in darkness.

"Good," she said, lingering in the shadow. "This is working out better than planned. I couldn't be happier." Giving a gentle, loving pat to each of the men as she passed, she basked in their silent adulation of her prowess and villainy.

Elizabeth still couldn't see the cloaked woman. She wore a black hooded dress lined with pearls. Her dress was the height of French fashion with magnificent embellishment that flattered her trim figure. She moved as if gliding around them, examining them as prey. A purr of satisfaction escaped her as she caressed Elizabeth's beautiful face.

"Yes, I am very pleased."

"Who are you?" Elizabeth asked, instinctively pulling away from the woman's cool fingers.

"Why, I'm surprised you haven't figured it out yet. I do understand there was a lot to take in, with all that was going around with the neighbors, your own poisoning and all mayhem as of late. I could give you the benefit of the doubt that you weren't quite yourself these past few weeks, but what would be the fun in that?" she said.

"If you don't tell her, I will," Lincoln countered, knowing how to ruin her fun.

"Very well," she said and motioning for the light to be brought closer. The woman removed her hood and stood before Elizabeth with gleaming eyes, full of malice and treachery.

Elizabeth knew exactly who it was. There was no mistaking her. This was Gabriel's mother, for if there ever was a female version of her husband, she was standing before her.

Giselle Athelston was a beautiful woman with her dark features and bright blue eyes, coupled with her womanly figure, could make a man come in tow without difficulty. Her innate badness, though, spoiled her outward beauty, therefore ruining her for anyone with goodness. No, she was not good enough for Lincoln or even her own son.

"Ah, I see your understanding. Perhaps things are becoming clearer for you?" Giselle asked.

"No, I don't understand. Why are you doing this?" Elizabeth begged.

"Money is the only reason she does anything," Lincoln said, resigned in her only motive.

"You have kidnapped us for money?" Elizabeth asked incredulously.

"Yes, dear, money. It is what makes the world go round. It also is what makes me happy. Money, money, and more money. You never can have too much, you know. Just ask King Henry."

"Don't be fooled, Elizabeth. She's broke. She hasn't a shilling left to her name after running off with everything we had. That is the only reason she's here," Lincoln revealed, gaining him a backhanded slap from his ex-wife. Her blow didn't deter him from continuing to reveal her true reason for kidnapping them. "She doesn't want just a little money, she wants as much as she can from wherever she can get it."

"What does that have to do with me?" Elizabeth asked.

"You, my dear, are bait. You see, Lincoln will not be around long. I have made sure of that," she said, smiling over at the butler. "Gabriel is to stand to inherit this property and the funds to go along with it. You are here to ensure that he hands it over to me. He probably doesn't want it anyway," she said, waving off its significance as if it were a trinket of little value.

"But you can't get away with something like this. Your criminal acts will land you in the stocks!" Elizabeth bit back her anger at the ruthlessness of this woman.

"I doubt it. I spread enough speculation around that no one will even suspect me. Take for instance, those little keepsakes you had that were used in destroying the Colhoster's forge mill and the Hessencastle's servant's living quarters. Wesley, here, has provided me with more than enough fuel to add to that fire with his adolescent crush, obsession really. Did you know he built a shrine for you in his bedroom? I take the startled look on your face that you didn't. Tomorrow, a letter shall be delivered to your father telling him that Wesley had run off with you and demands payment of an exorbitant amount or your life will end in poverty and your reputation ruined. He'll pay the sum and I will be all the richer."

"What about me and my mother?" Wesley asked, blatantly fighting against his bonds.

"Oh, don't you worry your young little mind over it. You'll end up with your precious Elizabeth in the end and your mother will get what she wants. When this whole fiasco is over, our husbands will be dead and we'll have all the money we need to live a good long while," she said gaily.

"What?" Elizabeth gasped at the pure wickedness she was hearing.

"Well, I have to protect my family!" Giselle said as a matter-of-fact. "What, did you not know that Lilith and I are sisters? Well, half-sisters, but regardless, family."

"I'm curious, Giselle, tell me how can children not be considered family?" Lincoln asked, equally disgusted at the woman's madness over money.

"My goodness, Lincoln, I'm not going to kill him, I'm just ransoming his bride," she batted her eyes as if she thought she was perfectly in her right to make demands and manipulations. "We have to go now. There is far too much to be done."

The three sat in stunned silence as Giselle left with her two henchmen leaving the three in total darkness once more. Elizabeth felt herself falling into despair. Her father was going to be killed for his money and his properties, all to fulfill Giselle and Lilith's greed.

Gabriel returned to the house after investigating the explosion, he knew instantly that it had been a diversion. Elizabeth and his father were gone. His mind went into full investigatory mode, analyzing every possibility. Chills ran down his back when he found a lamp on the floor with blood at its base.

His horse brought Bernard, the explosion brought many more. They all worked feverishly through the night to find them. The darkness stunted their search, eternally frustrating Gabriel. They had to wait until dawn.

"We know that there aren't any places to hide within the castle. They must have been taken elsewhere. We'll canvass the gardens until we reach the trees, then we'll systematically search every nook and cranny until they are found," Gabriel said, hoping to find tracks that would lead straight to them.

They searched meticulously through the gardens, in outbuildings, even moving solid ornaments for possible hideaways without success. It was midday before they reached the forest. Eager to press forward, Gabriel gave the command to extend the search into the trees.

"Lord Athelston," a young boy shouted to him, waving his arms wildly while atop his mule. Gabriel's frown grew deeper as he read the note the boy brought him. Without a word he made haste back toward Listenshire.

"We received this note just an hour ago. I thought you might wish to read it," Lilith said, handing him the note. Edward sat in his chair with the customary port clutched in his hand and the bottle tucked under his arm for safe keeping.

Gabriel read the letter with barely a cursory glance, folded it and placed it in a pouch tied at his side before quitting the room.

"Do you not care what they are doing?" Lilith called out after him.

"I beg your pardon, Lady Hollingberry. I don't explain myself to your kind," he spat back snidely.

"Humpf, I dare say, no man talks to me that way. Edward, call him back and make him tell us what is going on!" she cried to her drunken husband who was not so inclined.

"That was quick," Bernard commented upon Gabriel's return to his horse. Gabriel's response was handing the letter over to Bernard. "Well, we can add kidnapping for ransom to his list of crimes."

"Something isn't right Bernard. I can feel it," Gabriel said as they traveled back toward Laughtonwood. His determination to find Elizabeth and his father had not been extinguished with this find.

"We know that Wesley has the knowledge of chemicals and an unhealthy desire for Elizabeth. Why can we not assume that this note isn't proof positive?"

Gabriel thought about Bernard's question but only for a second before he put the two together. Taking the letter from the head master and the note he just received, comparing them side by side, he knew what was wrong.

"I knew it, Bernard! These two were written by the same person. Look at the handwriting. I know it isn't Elizabeth's, I would recognize hers. There has to be someone else involved."

"The writing is of someone educated. It also has a feminine scroll. What if Lilith wrote it? From what you have told me, she would support this venture."

"If it is, then I want her to think that I am oblivious. I want to find Elizabeth and deal with Wesley first."

"Sir, I found something."

Chapter 27

"**A**RE YOU CLOSE?" Elizabeth asked Wesley as he tried to manipulate his hands through the rope.

"No closer than I was an hour ago," he said, continuing to strain against the pain of his cut flesh.

"Neither am I," she replied, desperate to get free and save her father.

"Aha," Lincoln declared, surprising himself with his success. "Whoever tied me must have either felt pity for my weakened state or thought I didn't need as essential security. I'm free!" After regaining feeling in his arms, Lincoln attempted to feel how Elizabeth's restraints were configured. "I'm sorry, but without light there is no hope of understanding these knots."

"Try finding a rock or something sharp," Elizabeth suggested.

"I'm free too," Wesley shouted. He quickly doffed his bonds only to disappear into the dark.

"Wesley!" Elizabeth called out, just to be hushed by Lincoln.

"You don't want to raise alarm. Let's just get you out of these things and find our way out."

"Please hurry, for I feel he's going to bring us more trouble," she cried, feeling frustrated and abandoned.

"No, I'm not!" Wesley's voice sailed out of the darkness. "When they brought me in I remembered a pile of rocks that might have a sharp angle. I think I found one."

"Oh, bless you son." Lincoln said, feeling ultimately worried at their future if they had been caught, or even worse-if they had to leave her behind to fetch help.

It took several minutes and a few cuts to Elizabeth's skin to saw through the ropes with the inadequate rock, but Wesley worked diligently until the task was completed.

"Come quickly, we have to get out of here before they return," Wesley said. "Take my hand. We'll follow the wall until we reach light."

"Wait, I think I see light. Is it moving?" she asked.

"We are too far in for it to be anything else. We have to hide."

"You didn't have to come, Giselle. We could have taken care of feeding them ourselves," Thomas said.

"Nonsense, my dear, I would like to look at them once more before we move forward. Besides, it is on our way to Caprington where we launch our next campaign. It wouldn't do to have our mining aspirations stunted by property boundaries, would it?" she asked. Secretly she wanted to see her captives in their weakened state, especially Lincoln who kept her from fulfilling her life's ambition to be in high station. Now that she has acquired it on her own she had another desire-to watch him suffer.

"Look! They've escaped!" Thomas said, holding the lamp high over the empty chairs and the ropes that bound them lying on the ground.

"You imbeciles!" she screamed as she swatted at both men. "You didn't tie them tightly enough. Find them!"

"I hear water," Elizabeth said as they ventured further and further into the darkness. Having lost sight of the light behind them, they followed the wall hoping to find an exit but all they found was more darkness.

"Yes, so do I. That is a good sign, I think. It could mean that we are closer to above ground than we think," Wesley said.

"It sounds like a stream of water flowing," she said, hoping for a chance to escape.

"Keep listening. We'll head toward the sound and maybe find a way out," Lincoln suggested, holding fast to Elizabeth's hand.

"Five passages," Giselle said incredulously.

"Yes, they hit several voids and had to change direction," Thomas explained, trying to ascertain any footprints in the rubble. "They could be in any one of these caves. Let's split up."

"No, I have a better idea. They are most likely in the far left or far right tunnels. They have no light to see. They had to be following the wall," Giselle said.

"Yes, I think I see footprints along this wall," Mark pointed out and went headlong into the darkness.

"I see a glow up ahead," Wesley said, hoping it wasn't his hopeful imagination growing in the darkness.

"So do I and the flow of water is getting closer," Elizabeth clutched both of the men's hands as they walked faster toward the glow.

The pool of water had an ethereal blue-green glow, murky with the white ground stone the tunnel was excavated for.

"There has to be an opening somewhere, for there is light making the pool glow. I'll check it out," Wesley said, stripping himself of his jerkin and boots.

"No, Wesley, it's too dangerous. You could drown," Elizabeth cried.

"Don't worry, I'm a strong swimmer," he said just before diving into the water. It felt like forever waiting for Wesley to resurface. Elizabeth and Lincoln kept staring into the pool wishing him to show himself.

"I hope he finds a way out, but on the other hand I don't," Elizabeth said.

"Why ever not?" Lincoln asked.

"I can't swim."

"Well, then, it will be more believable that you committed suicide by jumping into the water out of a stricken conscience then, wouldn't it?" Giselle commented, spinning the others around in surprise. She chuckled as Lincoln placed himself in front of the chit. "Highly unlikely Sir Athelston. You couldn't even protect yourself, let alone another person."

"Let her go, Giselle. She doesn't deserve to be manipulated by you," Lincoln said bravely.

"But I'm not manipulating her, I'm manipulating her family and friends," Giselle said with a scolding purr.

"Friends? What have you done?" Elizabeth asked in morbid fear.

"I've broadened my horizons, dear. I have set my sights on Caprington property and I'm going to get it. There is too much emotion in a household. Memories of celebrations, of weddings, of fond memories with friends and families tied up into one's domicile. All one needs is one tragic memory to be tied in and POOF, there goes the attachment, and there is nothing more tragic than the death of a child."

"It's a mine. It looks like they are harvesting limestone. We've just found the arsenic source. It would take someone with a good knowledge of alchemy to separate it out, but it can be done. There is plenty here that would keep them in study supply," Bernard surmised.

"Search the caves men!" Gabriel shouted, being the first to charge into the dark cave.

It wasn't long before three empty chairs were found as well as multiple footprints leading further into the caves. Following them further and further, they soon heard angry voices then a scream. Gabriel rushed toward the sounds only to be stopped short.

Giselle Athelston, whom he hadn't seen in almost twenty years, was standing before him as his father lay dying from a dagger to the chest. Dismissing his mother, Gabriel went to his father's side.

"I'm sorry, father," Gabriel said remorsefully.

Lincoln's garbled words were masked by the blood filling his lungs. He couldn't push the words out, to tell his oldest son how proud he was of him and that he always loved him. Instead, the only thing he could do was force out one word. "Elizabeth," he said, forcing his arm to point toward the water.

"Elizabeth! Elizabeth! Don't die on me now!" Wesley said, shaking her and screaming at her to wake. He had just resurfaced after finding a way out when the dagger was thrown. It was aimed at Elizabeth, but Lincoln had jumped in the way, receiving the blow to save her. Wesley had to pull Elizabeth into the water, away from Lincoln and those who wanted to kill her.

Wesley had forced Elizabeth into the water in order to spare her life and swam as fast as he could, pulling her through the long tunnel until they reached the other side. Now, she lay lifeless. His rescue attempt failed. Crying unabashedly over killing his one love, he left her at the bank to get help.

Gabriel wasted no time diving into the water after Elizabeth. He swam until reaching the pond on the other side. He immediately spied Elizabeth's supine body. Rushing to her side, he quickly pushed the water out of her lungs, willing her to breathe.

The first gasp for air came in gulps, starving for it as she drew it in by the mouthfuls. Realizing who was holding her, she began to cry.

"I thought I would never see you again," she cried.

"Don't worry, I've got you now."

"Oh no, your father and mother," she cried, recalling what happened.

"Yes, I know. My men have everything under control. Don't talk now. I have to get you somewhere dry and warm."

Gabriel carried her to a nearby small cabin. He laid her on the bed and built a fire in short order. She stripped down to her chemise and draped her clothes over a chair close to the fire to dry and warmed herself the best she could.

"Why the blush?" he asked as she turned her back as he removed his own wet clothing. "After all, we are married."

"Yes, I know," she said, allowing Gabriel to escort her to the bed where she slid between the sheets. "It's just that there is more to this cabin than I care to admit."

"Please, tell me," he said teasingly as he lay beside her and gathered her into his arms, warming her with the heat of his own body.

"Philip had a mistress. This was where they carried on. More than likely he was going to see her when he returned from the Indies when he was assassinated. Perhaps he found the mine."

"Gently raised girls aren't supposed to know about mistresses," Gabriel gently scolded. "What is her name and how do you know about her?"

"Her name is Miriam Colhoster, William Colhoster's sister. Philip said that they had met years ago as young pups and fell in love. They kept their affair secret. The reason I know of her is that one day, while riding Majesty, I heard the bellow of a woman. Mistaking the sound as a call of distress, I rushed in not bothering to knock. She and Philip were-"

"Making love?" he concluded.

"Yes. But I didn't understand. I thought he was hurting her, so I tried to push him off to protect the woman." Elizabeth closed her eyes in mortification of the scene she could still see clearly so many years later.

"I see." Gabriel was hiding a smile, imagining a young girl coming upon such a sight. "Then let us change the memory for you," he said, holding her face in his palms, his long fingers reaching the back of her neck.

With conscious boldness, Elizabeth reached her lips to his and wrapped her arms around him to pull him down to her and reveled in the joy of it all. She loved the weight of him atop her, surprised that he didn't crush her although he was twice her size. She relished running her hands through his hair and over his back, mesmerized by the play of his muscles as he moved above her.

Gabriel had no compunction with removing the rest of his clothing, revealing himself to his wife. Nor did he feel ashamed as he led her to discover him. She quickly reflected his eagerness to reveal herself to him, letting him teach her the ways of love. She followed his lead as they intertwined, sharing their bodies and their love, allowing him to direct her, educate her, dominate her, love her body and soul. They were cocooned within their own world as they shared their love, making it complete in every way.

After many hours had passed, they awoke in each other's arms. He was regretting not waking earlier, but his concern waned as he looked down at Elizabeth, warmly snuggled under his arm and smiling up at him with a sleepy, but satisfied, grin.

"We must rise. Many will be looking for us," he said to her, brushing his lips across hers.

"Your senses have fled you, sir," Bernard said from outside the cabin. "We already know where you are."

Elizabeth pulled the blankets up over her head and blushed with embarrassment.

"I'll not have you behave that way, Lady Athelston. You are a married woman now." Gabriel scolded laughingly. "And just think, if I had given you that bedding party you requested."

"Yes, I agree. Privacy has many benefits," she said, recollecting the many things they had done with each other. She wouldn't have been so inclined if they'd had an audience.

"Please, rise and allow me to assist you, my lady." Elizabeth allowed Gabriel one more intimacy, allowing him to wash her intimate parts of the evidence of her ruptured maidenhead. He seemed pleased to assist her in this way. They quickly dressed and emerged from the cabin into the cool, crisp air of the morning.

"Good morning, mi'lady. I've taken the liberty to fetch your horse," Bernard offered the blushing bride. A dozen other soldiers stood at attention while he helped her mount.

"Thank you, Bernard. What of the others?" she asked.

"Sir Lincoln was regretfully killed in the tunnel. Wesley found us and lead us back to the pond where he left you. We followed you here."

"What will become of our captors?" she asked, watching Gabriel's face carefully.

"They will be sent off to the king's court to stand trial. He will see to their punishment," Gabriel said without any remorse over his mother's criminal cabal with Thomas Guiford and Mark Trembol.

"I think you might find it interesting to know that Giselle and Lilith are sisters. They were conspiring together," she said, filling them in on the rest of what Giselle had divulged. Gabriel reached over and brought Elizabeth onto his lap while they rode.

"Don't worry, my love. Everything has been set to rights now that we have Giselle in shackles."

Chapter 28

" S HE'S BACK AND *she's with* him," *she said, feeling the need to state the obvious. He said nothing in return but kept staring out the window as if daydreaming. "Well, aren't you going to do something? This is our last chance before he takes her away!"*

Still, he said nothing which only added to her ire. She stood and poked him with an unladylike finger until he looked at her.

"You aren't going to do anything, are you? I guess I'm going to have to do all the work," she said as she stomped off. She was not going to be put out without a fight.

"House arrest? How preposterous! I am a lady, Lord Athelston, and demand to be treated as such," Lilith demanded.

"You, Lady Hollingberry, are soon to be stripped of your title you so prize as soon as the king hears the case. An entire team of lawyers will not be able to defend your actions," Gabriel said with a level tone. He was not going to budge and she deserved no less.

"Edward, Edward!" she shouted out for her husband. "Oh, where is that man? At least let me visit with my son."

"I'm sorry, but I cannot allow that. He is under interrogation for his part in the past crimes. You will also be subject to answering my questions when I am through with him, unless you have something to say before I question him."

Lilith quietly refused to answer the barb, as if she was going to implicate her only son in any crime. She folded her arms and harrumphed, turning her chin up in derision.

Gabriel silently bowed out of the room and headed to the watchtower where the prisoners were being held. He marched in to where Wesley was shackled to the wall.

"How do you explain this, Wesley?" Gabriel ground out.

"What do you mean?" he asked, watching as Gabriel pull an item from his satchel, instantly recognizing it.

"I found these items in your room. They were set up on a pedestal, an altar if you will," Gabriel said, bringing each item out, throwing them on the ground as if they were refuse.

"No, No! You shouldn't have. Those things are sacred to me. She was going to be mine!" he blubbered.

"You've been obsessing over Elizabeth for quite a long time, haven't you? Only, when you went to make your move, the maid stood in your way so you removed her from the scene, didn't you?"

"No, I didn't. I was angry with her, yes, but I didn't do anything to her. The next morning, I took all the money I had and was prepared to bribe her, to give her the money to leave the house and live comfortably elsewhere, but she had already fallen down the stairs," he confessed.

"Can you prove it?" Gabriel drew, wanting to catch him in another lie.

"Yes, I'm sure of it. When I awoke, my curtains were opened. A servant must have seen me sleeping during that time, and before I retired I was in the study with my mother playing cribbage."

"I cannot rely on her testimony, Wesley, not when she has also been accused," Gabriel offered. Disregarding the boy's crestfallen look, he pressed him further. "What say you?"

"No, I have no other alibies," he said dejectedly.

"Hello, Papa. It's nice to see you out and about the grounds," Elizabeth said, noting the high pink in his cheeks. He's been drinking a lot lately and this morning was no different.

"Yes, the gardens are quite lovely with the changing of the color of the trees. Why don't we go for a ride, Elizabeth? It will be our last journey together before you go," he said, holding back the well of tears threatening to spill.

"I would love to," she agreed, gently taking his arm to test his stability. They walked to the stables reminiscing about their past jaunts and how much fun they used to have.

"Your sisters are due to arrive any day now," he said, lingering before the daunting task of mounting his horse.

"Yes, I know, and they will have to suffer the extremely simple wedding with just friends and family present. Simple but sufficient," Elizabeth said satisfactorily.

They rode alongside one another silently for a spell when Edward began speaking of Elizabeth's mother.

"Gwyneth was such a beautiful soul. Through and through, she was a true lady. She gave me five beautiful daughters and twenty of the best years of my life," he said as he wiped the tears from his face. "It pains me to not have been able to do anything in her hour of need."

"But you couldn't, Papa. The doctor and Marybeth both tried to help her and still could not," she consoled, taken aback by her father's display of such emotion, blaming the attack of conscience on the drink.

"I know, I know, deep down I know that I had no control over the matter. It just pains me so," he said with a loud blow into his handkerchief. "Shut-up," he said, swinging into the air as if to fend off an unseen assailant.

"Who are you speaking to, Papa?"

"No one, my dear, I'm just having a bit of a coughing spell."

"Charlotte, wake up. There are some men here to speak with you," Marybeth said as she assisted her daughter into s sitting position.

Gabriel felt pity for the girl. Her head was bandaged, large bruises hung below her eyes and she was lethargic.

"Please, I don't wish to cause her discomfort," Gabriel said watching the older woman prop her young battered daughter up with pillows.

"She'll be all right. I've been making her sit up a little each day. Please, have a seat." Marybeth produced a small stool and placed it beside the bed for him. "You will have to lean in closely if you want to hear her. She still speaks softly."

Gabriel took the proffered seat and gently took the girl's hand. Her eyes were clear but unfocused. He doubted if she was going to be able to tell him anything. It would be a miracle and a blessing if she returned to her normal state.

"Charlotte, my name is Gabriel Athelston and I am a guard of the king. I'm here to find out who did this to you. Do you remember anything?" he asked. They all waited patiently for an answer. Gabriel almost gave up until he saw a nod of her head. "Will you tell me who it was?" he asked, leaning in closely, placing his ear next to her mouth to catch what she would say.

"Yes, this is a beautiful sight. I recall attempting to paint is several times, but I don't have the skill yet to capture its essence or the truth of its meaning," Elizabeth admitted as the stood on the bluff overlooking Suffolk, the only home she'd ever known.

"I'm sure you would have grown into an amazing painter and done just that," Edward said, dismounting behind her.

"I'm still going to paint, Papa. I may be married, but that doesn't inhibit my desire to continue to paint," she said, hugging his neck as she had so many times before, "and I will always love you."

"Yes, yes, yes. I don't believe you and your promises, Elizabeth," Edward said in a harsh tone she had never heard before, let alone the shocking words.

"I beg your pardon?"

"You say you will always love me, but after breaking your last promise do you wish now to lessen the blow by saying you will always love me?"

"I don't understand. What other promise did I break and when did I break it?"

"You said that you would always stay with me and be near me when I needed you."

"Yes, I did, but Papa, I'm a grown woman. You should have known that I was bound to be married someday."

"So, you break your word to your father in his hour of need? How duplicitous! I see, since your handsome husband appeared you abandon all and leave everything and everyone behind to fend for themselves."

Elizabeth became increasingly confused by her father's ramblings and tried to not take offense at her dear father's words.

"Papa, you know that I had no say in the matter, neither did Gabriel. It was King Henry's doing that joined us!"

"How dare you throw this on someone else? You left me without so much as a goodbye!"

"Papa, you've gone mad!" she said, fearful for herself and him as well.

"Don't talk to him like that, you ungrateful chit! How dare you speak to him that way after all that he's done for you?" he said in a higher pitched voice.

"Please, Papa, let's go back home," she pleaded only to be pushed to the ground.

"Yes, let's go home," he said, drawing his sword.

Elizabeth held her breath as she searched frantically for a way to get off the bluff, then something happened that she couldn't quite explain.

"No, have you lost your mind? If you kill her you will be alone again, just like when Gwyneth left you."

"But then no one else can take her from me either."

"If you lock her away somewhere, maybe hide her until they stop looking for her, then you can have her all to yourself."

"You are too soft."

"But pragmatic! Take her to our favorite place and leave her there. No one will find her there. You'll see. It will be easy and no one will suspect."

"Really? No one?" Edward said with bitter-sweet realization.

"Trust me, who would suspect that you would hurt your dearest, youngest daughter?"

Elizabeth found herself shackled at the wrists and sitting on the dirt floor of a dungeon in an abandoned ruin a day's ride from Listhenshire. Her father sat across from her having another of his soliloquys. It was constant now, without letup and uninterruptable. She couldn't get through to him, no matter how she begged, no matter how much she cried.

"Papa, I'm hungry and thirsty. Please fetch me some water," she said meekly.

"No, it's too dangerous. They'll find you and then find her. It will only end badly. You've waited too long to return and now they will be looking for you, too."

"If you only go upstairs, perhaps finding a nearby well. It will be easy. No one knows where we are."

"Are you trying to trick him? His mind is not strong."

"What is your name?" Elizabeth asked out of boldness, realizing she wasn't the only one trapped.

"What are you about, Elizabeth? Why are you asking my name?" he said, as sober as he could be.

"I don't know, perhaps I'm at a loss for the sake of hunger." Elizabeth said weakly, hoping to fool the alternative personality inside her father.

"Let me peek out. Maybe there is nearby game."

"No you idiot! You must stay in hiding."

"But I am hungry too, Anglia."

"Don't make me wake up Charles. You know how you hate it when I wake up Charles."

"Why do you threaten me so? You know how distasteful it is to me!" he said, sitting himself down in defeat.

"Go to sleep, Edward. You need your rest. Tomorrow is coming soon."

Chapter 29

"DEVOTE ALL THE men to searching. I don't want a single stone left unturned. Go back through the mines again, inquire of the townsfolk again, do everything again!" Gabriel shouted, unable to control his frustration.

"Yes, sir," Justin said, leaving immediately to follow orders as quickly as possible to escape Gabriel's understandable disposition.

"What are you planning?" Bernard asked after following Gabriel to his horse.

"I'm going back to see if I can't track them."

"I'm going with you," he said, knowing fully that there were no discernible tracks to find.

They traveled to the bluff and searched below once more, following the trail until it grew cold once more, but he would not let his intuition be suppressed by practicality.

"I'm going on. They have to be out here somewhere. I may not be the greatest tracker, but I've got to try," he said, convinced that he would find her if he just went a little farther.

"Do we have a heading?" Bernard asked tentatively.

"We are going to Diss."

"Papa. Papa, it is raining," Elizabeth said, hoping for some relief. Edward woke with a snort and opened his eyes to see Elizabeth even weaker than the day before.

"Yes, I see," he said gruffly.

"If you have something to catch some rainwater, perhaps we can have a drink," she suggested.

Edward seemed to be mulling over the suggestion, or she was discussing it with his inner demons that seemed to control him more and more over the last three days. Without a word, he got up and walked feebly toward the stairs. Three days without drink was hitting him hard and Elizabeth could see its effect, but if she didn't get water soon she would die.

It took forever to gather the rain into the small bowl he'd found lying on the ground outside. He stood out in the dismal rain holding it until it had just enough to quench his precious daughter's thirst. Traveling downstairs was treacherous enough, let alone with a bowl of liquid. He reached Elizabeth with only half the water he'd set out with and looked upon her body.

"Look at her, Edward. Surely she has died."

"No," he blubbered, "that can't be true. She's just resting. She's weak from no food or water."

"You should leave her here. Only you know where she is. She will always be here when you need her, just as she promised."

"No Anglia. No! I cannot leave her. I shall stay with her until the end of days."

"Don't be a fool, Edward. Leave the water, leave this castle, leave her until you come back. Don't worry, I'll help you."

Edward's hands shook with the thought of leaving Elizabeth. Could he do it? Certainly he was not strong enough to do it on his own. Together, Edward and Anglia walked quietly over to where Elizabeth lay and placed the small wooden bowl of water beside her. They tiptoed toward the stairs, careful not to make a sound, but she stirred catching Edward's attention.

"Papa," she said in a lethargic voice. "Papa, give me a drink. I cannot reach it."

"Okay, my love." Edward complied, spilling half of it for of the shaking of his hands. He cursed himself for his ineptitude.

"It's all right, Papa. Thank you. Do you think you can find some food? I need my strength," she begged with a sweet smile.

"Can I find some food?" Edward asked, parroting the request as if in a stupor.

"Yes, my strength is waning. Please, Papa, I need food, perhaps something growing wild around the castle. Go look and see what you can find," she suggested.

"No, it's too dangerous. You took enough risk being out as long as you were fetching the water."

"But she is weak, just as I have grown weak," he argued, hearing nothing for a moment.

"All right, you forage for food, but eat your fill. She doesn't deserve to eat."

"She doesn't deserve it?" he repeated, flabbergasted at Anglia's conviction.

"Have you forgotten that she was leaving you for another man, another life far away from you? She was deserting you, Edward. Nothing good could have come of it."

"You are wrong, Anglia," Elizabeth said with as much strength as she could muster. "Something good can and has come from it. I am with child, Anglia. I am giving Papa a grandchild."

"A grandchild," Edward said cheerily as if he received the best gift ever.

"Yes Papa, a grandchild. If you let me live, I shall give you grandsons and granddaughters, enough to spoil to your heart's desire. I will surround you with them," she said, baiting his pride over the prospect of abundant family.

"Don't listen to her, Edward. She broke her promise to not leave you. What makes you think she will keep this one? Leave her!"

"Grandchildren," he said, liking the sound of it on his tongue and ignoring Anglia's unrelenting voice.

"Edward, are you listening to me?"

"Maybe you will have a girl and she will look like her grandmother. Will you name her after your mother, Elizabeth?" he asked, filled with hope and prospect.

"Yes Papa. That is a lovely idea."

"Stop listening to her, Edward. She will seduce you into letting her go. Leave her."

"Do you know what I remember most about Mama's death? It was that you never left her side. You held her hand and sat with her. You brushed her brow with a cool cloth and made sure she was comfortable."

"Yes, yes I remember that, too," he said forlornly.

"Please, Papa, let me live. Help me live like you wanted Mama to live."

"But I can't. They won't let me," he whispered.

"That's it. I'm waking Charles!"

"Oh no," Edward fretted and began to perspire. "Quick. We have to get out of here before Charles comes."

"We've come as far as Diss and haven't seen a single sign of them," Bernard lamented, sensing his commander's angst. "Do we move north?"

"No, they have to be here. I can feel it," Gabriel said, mulling over his tankard. "If we had brought more men, we could have canvassed Diss fairly quickly. Perhaps we missed something."

"What are you proposing?" Bernard asked.

"I want to circle around again, look from a different vantage point. The rain has let up. Let's go."

Gabriel was beyond frustration. With Elizabeth gone for three days, she could be anywhere. The possibilities made him even more exasperated. His gut was telling she was near, but all of his reasoning ability stated otherwise.

"Tell me, Bernard, what do you think? Where could Edward have taken her?"

"You know all the possibilities. I can't tell you any more than you already know."

"Maybe I'm too close to this one. I need more than my gut to rely on if we are going to find her," Gabriel admitted with a lump in his throat.

They made a wide circle encompassing Diss, looking at the landscape and searching for any tracks that may have been made by two horses. A mist began to settle over the earth, obscuring their view and dampening Gabriel's mood, making him doubt himself, doubt his judgment.

"Agrippa, go-" he started his command, then began thinking aloud. "Agrippa and Majesty have been housed together since we've been at Listhenshire, no? I don't know why I didn't think of this earlier! Agrippa, find Majesty," Gabriel commanded.

At first, Agrippa stood still, looking about from left to right trying to understand his master's command then slowly moved forward. They crossed a creek and traveled at least ten miles before coming to another stop.

Gabriel wasn't sure who heard it first, but the distinct sound of a horse in distress was clear. A high scream cut through the air followed by loud banging. Both master and stead reacted in tandem to the call. They followed the sound while fog settled around them, settling in to obscure their search.

Agrippa was on high alert with his ears perked and his eyes wide open, blowing huge billows of breathe, so when he stopped in his tracks, Gabriel was moved to dismount. To the horse's credit, they stood on the wrong side of what he believed to be a mote.

They had to travel afoot, following the edge to find a bridge for the sake of the risk of misstep by the horses, injuring them, all the while hearing the distressed horse's screams get further and further away.

"Here, I found a foot bridge," he called out to Bernard. Leaving the horses behind, the men followed the sounds once more.

Debris and stone were strewn about the place, with weeds and small trees growing within the cracks. They walked cautiously through the thick fog to finally reach the small outbuilding housing both horses. Gabriel opened the door to let the horse out and followed its lead.

"I'm sorry, girl, but I cannot see beyond my hand. Where is Elizabeth?"

"Listen," Bernard said, straining to hear, somewhere off in the distance.

"What are you doing, Edward?" Charles asked, thoroughly angered at being aroused.

"I'm not doing anything, go back to sleep Charles. Everything is under control," he said as he struggled to fish the manacle keys out of his pocket and fit it into the keyhole, shaking with the strain of it.

"That's not what Anglia said. She tells me that you have abandoned our plan, that you are abandoning us."

"No, no, I am doing nothing of the sort, I swear!" he said, dropping the keys onto the floor out of trepidation.

"You are lying to me, Edward, and you know what happens when you lie to me."

"No, I beg you, leave me be. I don't want to do this anymore," he blubbered.

"Do it quickly Papa. Do it quickly!" Elizabeth urged, knowing her father had a short grip on his own mind. She gently encouraged him to complete the task, but it seems Charles was too quick to act.

Edward, with no control over his own body, began pummeling himself, throwing himself around the room, into walls, onto the floor, doing any sort of damage possible. Despite Elizabeth's cries, the internal conflict continued. She begged and pleaded for him to stop, but to her horror, it only seemed to escalate.

"Elizabeth, Elizabeth!" she heard call.

"Down in the dungeon, please hurry!" she screamed, closing her eyes to the horrific scene happening before her. "Hurry, he's killing him!"

With a frantic search, they found cellar doors opposite the north wall. They entered and couldn't believe their luck. A large wooden door stood ajar leading to steps reaching far below.

Gabriel could see Elizabeth chained to the wall, crying with jerking sobs. As they reached the bottom of the stairs, he saw Edward's body sitting slumped in the corner, bleeding from many blows.

"Please, be careful with him. His mind is ill," she cried to Bernard, still unable to look at her father. She clung to Gabriel as he scooped her up and carried out of the dungeon. "Will you promise me we can find proper care for him?"

"Anything you wish, my love," he said, placing loving kisses all over her face. Climbing out of the dismal deep and into the grey mist, he quickly found a place to seat her for a proper inspection.

"You love me?" she asked, taking in the sight of his handsome face with her wide green eyes.

"Elizabeth Athelston, I think I have loved you from the moment we met," he said, gaining a prideful smile that quickly evolved into a deep kiss with promise.

"How did you find me?" she asked.

"Agrippa found you, or more to the point, Majesty who was making enough noise to wake the dead led Agrippa to this place," he said, lifting her up once more to carry her to safety.

"How long was I down there?"

"Three days," he said gravely, unable to assuage the feelings of guilt and self-displeasure at not getting to her sooner. "If I had only brought more men, I believe you would have been found sooner."

"Please don't blame yourself. Papa wasn't right. Even I didn't discern it until it was too late," she said, wishing to wipe the look of disappointment on his face. "I believe that, if I had realized earlier what Papa truly wanted, he would have let me go."

"What does he want?"

"Grandchildren and I promised him many," she admitted unabashedly. "I do believe this is the first time I've ever seen you smile," she said, liking it immensely. "It seems he isn't the only one hoping for progeny."

Gabriel carried her to his horse and mounted, unwilling to let her go for even a second. He stayed with her throughout the night and all of the next day, and ultimately placed her under guard whenever he had to leave her side.

Chapter 30

"MY GOODNESS, ELIZABETH," Taralyn gasped as she witnessed the goings-on before the ceremony, "I don't know how you can stand to think with all of these people around, little sister."

"I've grown accustomed to it. Actually, I've come to love it," she exclaimed excitedly, anxious to properly become the lady of the manor. "I'm so glad you could make it in time, Taralyn. When is the babe due?" she asked her beloved sister who had yet to show evidence of pregnancy.

"I think early spring. It is the best time to have a child," she glowed over the thought of the new life inside her. "Kathryn's boy is so adorable, I'm sure to be jealous if I have a girl. Martin predicts that it will be a boy, though," Taralyn said, fussing with perfecting the bow at the back of Elizabeth's dress.

"Then we will all three have boys as firstborns," she exclaimed brightly.

"Do you really think, I mean that you are also with child so early?"

"Yes I do, Taralyn, with all my heart."

"Then that is how it should be. I do believe you are ready, Elizabeth," she said, standing back to admire her sister's wedding gown their mother wore on her wedding day.

Gabriel stood before the priest, anxiously awaiting his bride to come through the doors. He'd arranged for Edward to attend, provided he be accompanied by the extra help they'd hired to care for the elderly man's needs for the sake of interference or a possible scene.

As he stood at the front of the chapel with the small group of family and scant friends, Gabriel found himself nervous, not for the fear of entering into matrimony to become encumbered, but anxious to move forward. He found himself reflecting on his life as of late and how vastly different things had worked out than he'd ever imagined.

A small smile of contentment crossed his lips as he recalled the last few days with Elizabeth and knew that his life would forever be changed. He was prepared to marry her, to dedicate his life to pleasing her. He wasn't prepared for the next round of emotions to assail him, though, as she walked in through the rectory doors.

Elizabeth wore a beautiful gown, her mother's wedding dress. It was made of fine brocade fabric, emerald green in color that matched her eyes. Gold embroidery adorned the bodice and sleeves, becoming more ornate at the neck, over the split sleeves and at the hem of the gown. The soft, wide sash of gold cloth was tied to a perfect, elegant bow at her back.

From the moment the chapel doors opened Elizabeth's eyes were trained on Gabriel. Standing next to her smiling father was her husband, her protector, her future, standing proud and tall with his chest out and shoulders back. He was so handsome in his black and gold wedding suit and an expression she couldn't define.

Gabriel couldn't take his eyes off her. She was more beautiful, more stunning than he ever imagined her being as she presented herself to him to become his wife before God and man. She willingly submitted herself to him and he couldn't have been more proud. A tear of mixed pride and admiration sprung into his eye as his heart swelled. Yes, his life was going to be very different than he'd originally planned. It would be better.

Time seemed to stand still as they exchanged vows, devoting themselves to each other. Sunshine streamed through the stained glass windows, Elizabeth's hands rested confidently in Gabriel's palms with love and surrender in her eyes as they listened to the priest declare their union as sacredly bound before God and all gathered, and peace settled all around them. Elizabeth declared that she would always remember this moment for the rest of her life, relating it to their future children as many times as they would stand to listen to it.

Gabriel surprised her with a firm embrace gathering her to him and a kiss that seemed too intimate for public, making her blush as they received whoops and whistles from his men. She knew that this wedding ceremony was more for show, for the people, but she felt it too. The king's edict bound them legally, but she truly felt she'd become a proper wife, presented before God and men alike as husband and wife to the world.

They made their way through the well-wishers, hand in hand, toward the baily where their carriage awaited them. They would begin their trek to Piffenview immediately, not delaying a moment longer. The bittersweet thought of starting her new life with Gabriel and leaving all her beloved family and friends behind made her tearful, clouding her thoughts as she stepped into the carriage.

"Stay put, my love. I have one last thing I need to do before we leave. Do you mind waiting for me?" Gabriel asked, placing a kiss on the back of his bride's hand.

"Yes, but do what you need. I'll be here waiting for you," she said, trying to withhold her tears of joy and sorrow that warred within her.

"Don't worry, Lord Athelston, I'll wait with her," Marybeth offered with a kind smile.

"Of course you will," Gabriel said. Marybeth was Elizabeth's nurse and would most likely needed to say good-bye, seeing her off into the next part of her life. Gabriel assisted Marybeth into the carriage and made his way to the watchtower.

Giselle and her thugs, along with Lilith and Wesley, were all placed under guard within the watchtower where Gabriel was set to leave them before they could be taken to the king for a judicial decision. Despite his desire to mete out retribution, he felt it would be more suitable coming from the king. King Henry VIII would not be easily swayed by emotion or family connection, neither would he put up with the likes of these misfits nor treat them kindly for plotting against one of his men, let alone wreaking havoc in his realm.

Unfortunately, though, something nagged Gabriel that kept his thoughts returning to the miscreant boy that attempted to foul Elizabeth and her good name. He recalled Wesley's stance when confessing his affair with Elizabeth, but couldn't seem to take advantage when given multiple opportunities. Gabriel decided to investigate if only to fulfill his own curiosity.

Wesley was brought out in shackles at his wrists and ankles like a hardened criminal. He was dirty and disheveled with straw in his hair and no shoes on his feet. He was pushed along by a guard that could care less of Wesley's comfort, forcing his hands above his head to be chained to a post to make escape impossible while out of arm's reach.

"Why have you brought me here?" Wesley asked snidely, clearly agitated with the man who summoned him.

"What relationship do you have with Giselle Athelston?" Gabriel asked. He wanted to get this over with as soon as possible and make his way to Piffenview with his new wife.

"Besides being my aunt, there is no relationship. I've only just recently met her. Why do you ask?" Wesley asked, knowing that Gabriel would use any and all information to pronounce him guilty of the crimes of his family.

"Are you telling me that you knew nothing of the plot against Listhenshire, to rob it of its value, divest it of peace and degrade its owners for the purpose of greed?" Gabriel ground out.

"I was not made aware of the scheme until the last," he said with a sneer.

"Perhaps it is because they knew you couldn't be trusted," Gabriel barbed, not sparing his own prejudice for the boy. "Children are usually kept ignorant of the activities of the parents, for the sake of secrecy."

"I am not a child," Wesley bit back.

"Oh, but you are, Wesley. Only a man would know the difference between molestation of a girl you find yourself infatuated with and making love with a woman. A real man would also not sully the reputation of a gently-raised lady either. You were afflicted with the same sickness as your kin. You wanted what was not yours to take and used treachery to attain it."

Wesley refused to acknowledge his guilt. He boldly stared into Gabriel's eyes, daring him to mention the name of his love. He knew in his heart that Elizabeth was his forever. Since that day he declared his love to her in the woods, the day he'd fallen completely and utterly in love with her, completely consumed by her, he vowed that she will always be his. Their kind of love was undying, never to be replaced by another.

"Elizabeth is mine and always will be," Wesley said as if it were a statement of fact. "We share something special, something that can never be denied. I love her and she loves me. She said as much with everything she did. She is my queen, she is my life-mate, she is my moon and stars, she is-"

"She is my wife," Gabriel cut in. He was ready to be rid of this boy and there was only one way to do it. "There can be no denying it, Wesley. She will never be yours."

"What is that?" Wesley asked as Gabriel produced a stained cloth.

"This," Gabriel ground out, "is proof of my wife's maidenhead."

"No, it can't be," he panted, refusing to believe such a thing but was unable to take his eyes away from the bloodied cloth. "You're lying."

"No, Wesley. It is you that lied when you told me that you had an affair, that you seduced Elizabeth, that you had no part in the plot against her."

"Put it away, I cannot bear to see it!" Wesley cried, only to have the cloth brought closer to him.

"Why, Wesley? Is it because you couldn't do it? Is it because you couldn't follow your mother's direction? Or is it because you can't stand the fact that she belongs to someone else, to me, and that I rightfully claimed her as my wife?" Gabriel spat.

"She betrayed me," Wesley finally said, shaking with his fury. "I was trying to protect her, but she betrayed me instead. All of the schemes, all of the plans, they were all so secretive, but I knew. I knew."

"You know nothing!" Gabriel taunted.

"I knew, I overheard them talking about getting the house upon the death of Sir Hollingberry. They were going to do away with Elizabeth so there would be no question of ownership after her father dies. I tried to protect her. We were going to marry and move away and she would be safe," Wesley whimpered as hot tears rolled down his cheeks. "That is, until Giselle and mother got wind of it."

"From whom were you saving her?" Gabriel asked as his hairs stood on end.

"Don't you know? The 'Great Guard of the King' who can deduce even the hint of conspiracy doesn't know who the true criminals are?" Wesley laughed in his face, seemingly delighted at Gabriel's expense. Finally, Wesley had the upper hand. He felt powerful in knowledge and with the anguish he was causing this man who was the bane of his existence.

"Tell me now. Who wants Elizabeth dead?" Gabriel ground out. Wesley only laughed in his face in reply. "As God as my witness, if anything happens to her I won't wait for King Henry to pass judgment. I'll kill you myself."

"If I can't have her, then no one will," he said with resolve.

Chapter 31

"I'M SORRY, LADY Athelston, but we must move to make way for the troupe behind us. I'll just move us beyond the gates," said the liveryman.

"Alright, just make sure that Gabriel knows where we are," she said before turning her attention back to Marybeth. "To answer your question, yes I am very excited. Even though I loath to leave Papa behind in his condition, it can't be helped."

"Don't fret, my dear. We'll take good care of him. Even though his mind has gone awry, he may still live a long while. I'll let you know if there is need to return," Marybeth said kindly, watching as they passed out of the baily and toward the outer gates.

"Is it just me or is this carriage rocking a bit more than usual?" Elizabeth asked with a hand on her belly and a piqued look on her face.

"Perhaps you may be right about a babe coming. Your mother was always sick right away after conception. Here, take a nip of this. It will calm your troubles." Marybeth watched as Elizabeth did as she was told, smiling that all was not lost. They could still recover their losses while they had the chance.

"Thank you, Marybeth. I am so grateful for you and all you have done for me. I think I will miss you most, even more than Charlotte and Darwin," Elizabeth crooned, knowing there wasn't any time left to say the things she had in her heart.

"Please, Miss Elizabeth, that isn't necessary. I'm a paid worker, that is all," Marybeth said with a bit of discomfit, fidgeting in her seat.

"Nonsense, I give credit where credit is due. I think of you more than just an employee. You have been with our family through thick and thin and I hope you felt the measure of love each of us girls has for you," Elizabeth said, disregarding Marybeth's uneasiness, resolving to share her feelings as she departed for her new life so far away from her childhood home and all that went along with it.

"I suppose that is the plight of all ladies moving on and becoming wives and mothers. This attachment to nurse-maids cannot be helped, but I am no longer your nurse-maid," Marybeth said sternly, all too aware that they had past the gates and have continued on.

"Don't you feel sorrow with each chick that leaves the nest?" Elizabeth said, finding herself oddly tearful and emotional. Fatigue set in and she leaned against the bolstered carriage wall and closed her eyes.

"This is a bit different, Elizabeth," Marybeth said as Elizabeth drifted into a strange fog.

"What have you done Marybeth? Why did you poison me again?" she asked in a lethargic voice.

"I didn't give you poison this time Miss Elizabeth. We need it to look like an accident," she said, trying to keep the remorse out of her voice. She really was going to miss the chit.

"But why?" Elizabeth managed to ask despite the overwhelming fatigue robbing her body of the will to stay awake.

"Because you didn't die the first time I poisoned you. It would have been all too easy to lay the blame elsewhere, but things don't always turn out as planned. At least now I'll make sure that the job is done properly." There was no turning back now. The plan was set in motion as the driver barreled toward the bluffs in a dead run.

Panic set in as Gabriel raced into the baily where he'd left his new bride only to see the carriage missing. There was no time for Wesley's games. The extra time he took to force a confession out of Wesley proved very useful, but only if their ploy hadn't yet been carried out.

"Cabrara and Pecor, gather the men. Elizabeth has been kidnapped," Gabriel said, not waiting for the command to be fulfilled before mounting Agrippa and speeding toward the outer gates.

Gabriel caught sight of the speeding carriage and bolted after it. They were more than half-way to the bluffs as he surmised their intent. Fear gripped him, squeezing his heart as he contemplated losing Elizabeth.

Fear, determination and pure desperation spurred him on, pushing himself and his horse harder to gain speed. Sweat poured down his brow as he pushed even harder when both the maid and the driver jumped from the carriage, allowing the carriage to careen toward the deadly drop unmanned.

There was no room for failure. His men were too far behind to assist him. He had to stop the carriage before it reached the bluff. The horses continued despite the loss of their driver. His only hope was to slow the carriage down enough to gain control of the team of four.

Thinking quickly, Gabriel took hold of his mace and threw it, catching it within the spokes of the back wheel. The carriage slowed minimally, but it slowed, giving rise to hope. Next he threw his sword, but it ricocheted off the wheel, coming back at him and nearly piercing his horse. His short sword and axe were next, slowing the carriage even more.

Finally able to reach the lead horse, Gabriel tried to turn the team away from their path. The frenzied horses fought hard against him as the lead horse unexpectedly reared up causing the carriage to stop suddenly and topple over onto its side with a crash.

Gabriel wasted no time getting to Elizabeth. Her limp body lay crumpled on the side of the carriage, lifeless and bleeding from her head. He climbed in after her as his men unhitched the still-frantic horses.

"Elizabeth, Elizabeth, please wake. Tell me that you are all right," he pleaded, kissing her face and caressing her hair until her eyes began to flutter.

"Yes, I think I'm whole. What happened?" she asked, confused from the position she found herself in.

"I'll explain later," he said, breathing a sigh of relief. Gathering her up and lifting her out of the carriage she was meant to die in, Gabriel carried his bride toward his horse eager to get her away from Suffolk and the dangers within.

"No," came a bitter scream, "you are supposed to die!" The woman declared. Gabriel's men had detained her, placing her under immediate arrest along with the driver. "You were supposed to die, I say! Why won't you die?" Marybeth screamed, thrusting against the grip of her sentries.

"Why do you wish to see her dead?" Gabriel demanded.

"All ties with this family were severed when you sacrificed my daughter. She will never be the same," Marybeth screamed in anguish. Rage and tears streaked her face as she raised a fist into the air in revolt. "It is the only way for us to earn security. Sir Hollingberry willed all his servants to inherit everything, provided Elizabeth does not survive him."

"Servants cannot inherit," her captor stated matter-of-factly.

"Yes they can, I say that they can! Look at his will. You will see that he made the will well before his mental state appeared. You can't change it now! It will stand up in court! You can't change it now!" she argued.

"Marybeth, how could you do such a thing? You have been so good to the family, so good to me, especially since mother died," Elizabeth asked.

"And what of you, may I ask. My daughter sacrificed herself for you, possibly remaining damaged for the remainder of her life, yet you go on living as if it never happened."

Knowing full well that she didn't have to replay to the servant, Elizabeth dignified the long-time servant's claim with an answer anyway. It was the least she could do for the bald pain that was in Marybeth's eyes.

"I'd made arrangements for you and Charlotte to come to Piffenview after she was deemed fit to travel. She is in no such condition now. It would be unconscionable of me to ask that of her, risking her life. I have too much respect for her to ask that, and too much respect for life. She showed her fealty to me the day she was injured. I have always planned to show her that same fealty."

Marybeth was taken aback. She couldn't imagine such reciprocity for her daughter, her precious, injured daughter. Shock showed on her face as she abandoned her struggle against her captors. Elizabeth, with whom she'd been at her beck and call since the day she was born, had never been overly demanding nor unfair with any servant, had made arrangements to take care of them. Marybeth allowed the knowledge to massage her heart.

"Truthfully?" she asked with tears in her eyes.

"Yes," Elizabeth said, fully intending to carry through with the promise, at least toward Charlotte who she was sure had no part of this devious plot.

Marybeth relaxed in defeat as she was escorted out of the ruins of the chapel. She turned toward the castle that was her entire life, her home, her sanctuary. She was born here and she knew she wanted to die here. She stopped and took a deep breath, filling her lungs with its air.

As tears of remorse filled her eyes and regret filled her lungs, she turned and headed toward her doom with resolve. The driver had other plans as he fought against his captors only to be knocked down for his misbehavior. A moment later, a hidden dagger was produced and hurled at Elizabeth.

Unable to bare Elizabeth's demise Marybeth leapt and landed with a crash as she caught the blade in her mid-section as another blade sliced through the air. Bernard had seen the dagger at the last moment. Unfortunately, he wasn't able to react quickly enough for Marybeth who sacrificed herself for her mistress.

Elizabeth, baffled by the totality of the corruption surrounding her, cried in Gabriel's arms over the loss of her home and those she loved. Yes, things turned out far different than he could have ever imagined. He also gave thanks to God for the king and Sir Otholomew intermeddling in his life that allowed him to find Elizabeth and save her from such destruction.

Not permitting her to remain one minute longer, Gabriel escorted Elizabeth out of Listhenshire Hall's reach and carried her toward Piffenview where she would be safe and secure in his arms for as long as he shall live.

With that promise, his private vow to keep her safe and loved, Elizabeth never found herself alone at night, nor far from him throughout her days.

Epilogue

"PAPA," GWYNETH SAID, sitting atop her father's lap. Her dark hair and green eyes shone brightly as she made to ask her father for something.

"Yes, my dear. What is it?" he asked his only daughter of six children with the seventh on the way.

"I'm ten years old now, don't you think I need a hobby?" she asked in her own feminine way. Gwyneth had always been a pristine, utterly feminine child, preferring to play with dolls rather than getting dirty in any shape or form.

"Why do you ask?" he returned, wondering what she would come up with.

"Well, Frederick trains falcons, William spends his time hunting, Kirby likes to invent things, and Michael has just took an interest in building things, heavens knows what it will turn out to be, though. Clifton is just a babe, so he doesn't count."

"I see, so you feel left out, do you?" he asked, knowing full well that she has more than she needs to keep her occupied.

"Yes. I need a hobby, something to keep my mind busy-except with lessons. Something that will help me to become rounder," she said in her most grown-up voice.

"Do you mean well-rounded?" he corrected.

"Yes, that is what Miss Charlotte tells me. She said that the boys are growing up and becoming more independent, finding their true callings and I want to have a calling of my own," she said, feeling she's missing out on fun everyone else is having.

"Gwyneth, it isn't that easy. You can't have someone tell you what you like, you have to figure that out for yourself," Elizabeth said, who was sitting across from them.

"How will I know what that is?" she asked, fully intending to receive a direct, easy answer to her problem.

"You won't know until you find out for yourself. You have to try many things until you find that one thing you like best," Elizabeth replied, receiving a scrunched up, disagreeable face for her effort.

"Why don't you start making a list of thing you would like to try and do them? You can cross them off one by one as you complete them to your satisfaction and then you can have an informed decision," Gabriel suggested.

"Where do I start?" she asked, completely exasperated with the task already.

"You can try doing things others know how to do. You can ask one of your brothers to teach you their hobby, or you can ask your mother to teach you hers," he said.

"Mama's?" she said quizzically.

"Yes, what is wrong with that, my dear?" Gabriel asked, trying to discern what was in his daughter's heart.

"Mama's hobby is to make babies and take care of us," she said innocently, confused by her parents' laughter.

"No, dear, what he means is that I paint pictures. Maybe one of these days you will want to learn," Elizabeth explained, trying to contain her laughter for the sake of the girl's feelings.

"Oh," Gwyneth said, thinking it over. "I'll go think about it and make my list." Jumping down from her father's lap, she left the room without a backward glance.

"Well, I have to say that her first guess was true," Elizabeth said, caressing her swollen abdomen. Gabriel came over to her, kneeling before her and boldly kissed her stomach. "Gabriel!" she said, thoroughly embarrassed by his brazen act in the light of day.

"I was going to say that baby making was my hobby, not yours," he said, still hungry for her after all these years.

"And you are mighty good at it, I must say," she confessed after a quick glance around the room.

"Are you nervous that someone will catch us, my love?" Gabriel growled seductively.

"It is the light of day, husband of mine," she said, blushing even after all this time.

"Believe me, if we didn't carry on like this the servants would worry that something was amiss. We have to give them the benefit of knowing that their lord and lady are happily enjoying each other," he said convincingly as he made a trail of kisses toward her neck.

"What if one of the children catch us?" she asked, thoroughly distracted by Gabriel's attention.

"All the better. They will know that their parents love each other. Perhaps we should move this to another room," he suggested, standing and offering his hand to his still beautiful bride. Elizabeth accepted his hand with a look of scandal in her eyes and pink in her cheeks.

Acknowledgements

I COULDN'T GO without acknowledging many people who have assisted me in one way or another during the creation of this book. My family should be the first that should be thanked, since I was away from them for so long. I wrote this book during a very difficult time in my life. This creative outlet kept my mind busy as I cared for my father who was dying of cancer as I simultaneously went through registered nurse schooling in an accelerated program. I was "away" in more ways than one, but with my family's help I was able to cope during this time. I thank God every day that I have such a loving, devoted husband and two gracious children that understood that this cathartic exercise needed to take place.

I also need to thank Scott Bushnell, a wonderful journalist, who has more practical advice in his pinky finger than I have in my entire body. Scott graciously agreed to edit my first manuscript for me, not knowing I had such an issue with sentence structure or homonyms. He was kind in his delivery and gave me very honest-hearted direction. This quiet, gentle man is one that would benefit even the most experienced of writers with his literary knowledge. Freely dispensing his wealth of scholarly intelligence, he helped me realize a grander picture, the true definition of being a successful writer, and that there is always room for improvement. He even gave me a tutorial on how to execute a successful interview with the press, which later segued into a lesson in humility. He truly has the ability to build up without first tearing down. I enjoyed working with him and look forward to the possibility of working with him again in the future.

I would like to thank those at iUniverse that worked well with me and gave me constructive criticism that allowed me to grow as a writer and envision being more than just a writer, but a better thinker as well.

To the gentleman that wishes to remain anonymous that recovered my lost files when I was more than half way through the manuscript, thank you for saving my sanity.

About the Author

J ANET BENNETT LIVES in Indiana with her husband and two children and has had a lifelong interest in writing. She is trained as a registered nurse and is also the author of the novel Hidden Treasure.